INNOCENT
IN HIS DIAMONDS.

BY
MAYA BLAKE

MILLS
& BOON

Published in Great Britain 2015
by Mills & Boon, an imprint of Harlequin (UK) Limited,
Eton House, 18-24 Paradise Road, Richmond, Surrey, TW9 1SR

© 2015 Maya Blake

ISBN: 978-0-263-24838-8

Harlequin (UK) Limited's policy is to use papers that are natural, renewable and recyclable products and made from wood grown in sustainable forests. The logging and manufacturing processes conform to the legal environmental regulations of the country of origin.

Printed and bound in Spain
by CPI, Barcelona

'Save the act, ___ ___ ___ ___ding outrage while your eyes devour me wears thin after a while,' he sliced at her.

'God, you are full of yourself, aren't you? The outrage is *real*. I've never met anyone more infuriating than you. And there's nothing remotely sexual about that!'

There—that should set him straight, she congratulated herself, so pleased with her comeback that she didn't acknowledge the charged silence until his hand landed on her shoulder.

'Then this shouldn't affect you too much.'

'Wha—?'

His lips slanted over hers before she could get the word out.

Ana's world imploded. Every coherent thought, every ounce of outrage fled as she experienced Bastien, up close and devastatingly personal.

His kiss started out as a ruthless lesson. Very quickly it became something else. Something that made her stomach muscles quiver.

His lips, hot and urgent, seared her, branded her, evoking such electrifying reactions that she could do nothing but cling on, crave more, open herself to the pleasure drenching her.

When his tongue stroked hers molten heat seared through her, singeing every nerve-ending, every drop of her blood, until she burned, engulfed in sensual flames.

Bastien had called her reaction to him an act. Except it wasn't an act. The world might think Ana Duval represented sex on legs, but the truth would shock them even more. The fact was that she was as far removed from being sexually promiscuous as was humanly possible.

Maya Blake's hopes of becoming a writer were born when she picked up her first Mills & Boon® aged thirteen. Little did she know her dream would come true! Does she still pinch herself every now and then to make sure it's not a dream? Yes, she does!

Feel free to pinch her too, via Twitter, Facebook or Goodreads!

Other titles by Maya Blake available in eBook from www.millsandboon.co.uk:

WHAT THE GREEK WANTS MOST
  (The Untamable Greeks)
THE ULTIMATE PLAYBOY
  (The 21st Century Gentleman's Club)
WHAT THE GREEK CAN'T RESIST
  (The Untamable Greeks)
WHAT THE GREEK'S MONEY CAN'T BUY
  (The Untamable Greeks)
HIS ULTIMATE PRIZE
MARRIAGE MADE OF SECRETS
FAKING IT TO MAKING IT
THE SINFUL ART OF REVENGE
THE SECRET WEDDING DRESS
THE PRICE OF SUCCESS

INNOCENT
IN HIS DIAMONDS.

CHAPTER ONE

BASTIEN HEIDECKER THREW open the doors of his boardroom and strode in. For several seconds none of his board members noticed his presence, absorbed as they were by the catastrophe playing out in high definition on the big screen.

Henry Lang, his CFO, spotted him first.

'Mr Heidecker! We were just catching up on the latest development…' The short dark-haired man grabbed the remote, pressed a button and dashed to his seat.

Bastien watched the rest of his staff scramble into their places, his already simmering anger mounting as his gaze shifted to the screen.

Her frozen image stared back at him. Despite the storm brewing beneath the surface of his calm, Bastien couldn't fault his team for being enthralled by the woman at the centre of the chaos engulfing his company.

Ana Duval was stunning perfection. The half-Colombian, half-English supermodel's beauty combined innocence and defiance with a hint of cultivated vulnerability that had been skilfully honed into the perfect commodity. That combination had ensnared every red-blooded male in the western hemisphere and ensured her a permanent place in the limelight by the time she'd turned twenty-one.

Hell, it had nearly ensnared *him*…

Even at fifteen Bastien had known the skinny, doe-eyed, eight-year-old he'd had the misfortune of spending that unforgettable winter with was nothing but trouble. What he *hadn't* foreseen was that sixteen years later Ana Duval would bring bedlam right to his doorstep.

His gaze skimmed the silky fall of her straight black hair, the slim, delicate structure of her lissom figure and the legs that had once been described by a fawning companion as forty-two inches of creamy paradise.

Against his will his body stirred in remembrance of having that body close to his only two months ago, of soft, meaningless words whispered in his ear.

He smashed away the memory, took his seat at the head of the table and focused on his second-in-command. 'What's the latest on the share price?'

He received a wary grimace. 'Less than half of what it was yesterday and still falling.'

'What are the lawyers saying? Can they make this go away?' he shot back.

Henry glanced down at his watch. 'There's a court hearing at two o'clock this afternoon. They're hoping since this is Miss Duval's first offence the judge will be lenient—'

'*Alleged* offence.' Bastien ground out the words.

Henry frowned. 'Excuse me, sir?'

'Until there's clear evidence to prove otherwise, this is merely an alleged offence, *non*?'

Other board members fidgeted. Henry's gaze darted to the screen. 'But she was caught on camera with the drugs in the VIP area of the nightclub—'

Bastien's lips compressed. He'd already seen the footage some enterprising fool had flooded the internet with on the way from Heathrow. So had the Geneva board members of Heidecker Bank—the largest, most elite private bank in the world and the mother company of Diamonds by Heidecker. Their reaction had reflected his own outrage. He needed to nip this problem in the bud.

He had the trust of most of the board, but the stigma never went away.

Like father, like son.

He was nothing like his father. He'd made it his mission since that dismal summer to prove to himself that sharing DNA didn't meant sharing deplorable traits. He'd succeeded for twelve years—until one small misstep two months ago had unearthed a doubt he hadn't been able to erase since. He'd given in to seductive words and an alluring body and he'd almost lost his focus…

He raised his gaze, stared at the culprit and struggled to keep his cool.

The likelihood of Ana's innocence was less than marginal, but he kept this to himself.

'Despite what the alleged evidence says, Ana Duval is the face of the DBH range. Our diamonds are worn by the wives of heads of state and A-list celebrities all over the world. Until she's categorically proved guilty her offences remain strictly alleged, and we'll do everything to promote that innocence—is that understood?'

Bastien waited until he received nods of agreement before rising.

The sense of *déjà vu* was overwhelming. The deep, unshakable notion of history repeating itself would have been laughable had he given it any thinking room. But for the sake of his company and his reputation he couldn't dwell on the past.

Ana Duval might look like a younger version of the woman who'd ripped his family apart, but he was not as weak as his father.

He had to stand by his employee. Distancing himself would only send a message that the allegations had teeth and sound a death knell to the Diamonds by Heidecker ad campaign.

'How are we handling the media?' he asked his senior press officer.

'We're taking the "no comment" route.'

He nodded. 'Maintain that for now. But draft a statement denying the allegations and send me a copy.' He turned to Henry.

'Send feelers out to our competitors. We have to be ready to sell the company if things keep heading south.'

He was first and foremost a businessman. Before this scandal the signature DBH brand of diamonds had held its own and even excelled in a saturated market. But he knew first-hand how scandal could rock even the safest, most solid foundation—destroy the strongest family.

'Isn't that a bit precipitate?' Henry asked hesitantly.

Across the gleaming surface of the conference table Ana Duval's dangerously captivating face stared back at him.

'Sometimes you have to cut out the threat of disease before it gets the chance to take hold and spread.'

Ana Duval rubbed her wrists. Memories of handcuffs closing over her flesh remained vivid and frightening more than twelve hours after the fact.

Even more terrifying was the judge's ruling. The preliminary hearing had been alarmingly quick, and the female judge had shown zero sympathy so far.

Ana jumped to her feet. 'Two hundred thousand pounds? I'm sorry, Your Honour, but that's—'

'Miss Duval! *We'll* handle this,' her lawyer said hurriedly as the judge paused and glared at her.

Ana fought not to cower. This whole thing was preposterous. Even if she sold everything remotely of worth in her life she would still fall hopelessly short. She sank back into her seat and rubbed her wrists again, certain that any minute now she'd be dragged back to that dank, soulless cell.

Beside her, the lawyers representing the Heidecker Corporation scrambled into a huddle. She let their voices wash over her and quickly calculated how much money she had in the bank. It didn't take long.

God, she was going to jail. For using her inhaler. An inhaler that had mysteriously vanished, to be replaced in her purse by another one filled with heroin. The absurdity of her situation would have been comical if it hadn't been so serious.

Watching her mother pop pill after pill at the slightest hint of unhappiness or adversity had instilled a hatred of substance abuse in Ana at a very early age. Only a very serious asthma attack a year ago had finally convinced Ana to carry her inhaler with her at all times.

Ironic that the very object that was supposed to save her life was what could now ruin it.

The lawyers finally stopped chattering. She opened her mouth to demand to know what was going on. And stopped.

The tingle invading her body was not unfamiliar. She hadn't experienced it in a long time. In fact— Her heart began a discordant hammer as she recalled the last time she'd felt like this.

It had been on her second day of shooting the first phase of the Diamonds by Heidecker ads. Reclining on the sun-washed deck of a super-yacht in Cannes, bored out of her mind, she'd wondered how soon she could get away to call her father and congratulate him on his latest archaeological find.

The tingle had started much like this one—easing its way up her toes, engulfing her ankles, her calves, weakening her knees, singeing the secret place between her legs. The tingle had stopped there, establishing an almost possessive hold, before rising to engulf her whole body.

Then, as now, she'd wanted to run, to hide and cover herself—a ridiculous notion, considering her profession more often than not involved flaunting herself. Finally, just when she'd felt light-headed from the sensation, the photographer had wrapped the shoot.

Uncoiling from her pose, she'd turned her head.

And had encountered the silver gaze of Bastien Heidecker.

What had happened afterwards still had the power to stop her breath, to raise her heart-rate to dangerous levels no matter how much she tried to downplay the memory.

She turned her head now and encountered the same piercing gaze.

The breath shot from her lungs and that unnerving tingling engulfed her whole body, turning it from numb to fiery within seconds. Her every nerve-ending screeched in awareness of the man whose gaze pinned her to her chair, imprinting and condemning all in one go.

She watched in silence as, without breaking eye contact, he strode to the lawyers and spoke in deep, low tones.

The lead counsel nodded and cleared his throat and Bastien turned towards her, his towering six-foot-two frame and confident tread causing heads to turn in the courtroom. He took a seat directly behind her and with an autocratic jerk of his chin ordered her to face forward.

Heat crawled up her neck, stung her cheeks. With it came anger at herself for so blatantly staring. The judge's gavel struck, making her jump. Glimpsing Bastien's mocking smile, she pursed her lips and straightened in her chair.

For the hundredth time Ana wished she'd insisted on changing her clothes before arriving in court. But she'd wanted this hearing over and done with. She glanced down at the thigh-skimming silk dress—already on the risqué side when she'd worn it last night to please Simone, her flatmate, and now bordering on the downright indecent in daylight, especially in a courtroom—and cringed inwardly.

She was discreetly tugging it down when the noise level rose. The lawyers were smiling and shaking hands with Bastien. Grabbing her tiny purse, she stood up.

She glanced around her and noticed there were no guards ready to slap the handcuffs back on and cart her off to jail.

'What's going on?' She'd aimed for brusque and businesslike but her words emerged thick and heavy, as if she were speaking in a foreign tongue. With a leaden hand she pushed back the heavy fall of hair from her face.

Bastien stepped forward, his grey eyes arctic-cold. 'Found it hard to concentrate, did you?'

'I beg your pardon?'

The breadth of his shoulders and the sheer force of his personality threatened to overwhelm her. Or it might be because she hadn't eaten a thing since yesterday. Whatever it was, the light-headedness when she looked into his eyes made her senses swim.

Strong hands gripped her arms and he swore under his breath. She pushed him away but he held on, his irritated growl sizzling along her raw nerves.

'You will be by the time I'm finished with you,' he rasped into her ear.

She shivered. That deep voice had intruded on her dreams far too many times, mocked her weakness when it came to Bastien Heidecker. At eight she'd followed him around like a puppy-dog, despite the *stay-away-from-me* vibes he'd projected loud and clear. At twenty-four she'd almost succumbed to a far more dangerous temptation that continued to haunt her.

No way was she letting that happen again.

'Let me go, Bastien.' She wrenched herself from his arms— only to find herself recaptured a moment later when his hands closed over her shoulders.

'I don't know whether anything can get through that drug-fogged brain of yours, but I suggest you try and understand this. We're going outside now. My car will be waiting, but so will the press. You will not say a single word. If you have the slightest inclination to do so, kill it. Do you understand?'

'Get your hands off me! You've got this wrong. I'm not—'

His fingers bit into her shoulders, stifled her protest. A shiver coursed through her as he hauled her closer, his body so close his scent surrounded her.

'If you want to get out of here in one piece the only word I want out of your mouth right now is *yes*.'

A rebellious fire lit her belly. For as long as she could re-member she'd relied on no one but herself. She'd had no choice.

But this—lawyers, court, the threat of imprisonment—was totally alien to her. Besides, deep down she'd known that she'd have to answer to Bastien sooner or later. He was ultimately her boss. She only wished it had been much later.

Swallowing her words, she nodded. 'Fine. But only until we get out of here.'

He pulled back, his unforgiving gaze raking down her body. His nostrils flared and she caught a spark of that dark and dangerous emotion that had arced between them on that sultry night two months ago.

With short, jerky movements he tugged off his jacket and settled it over her shoulders.

'Do my clothes offend you?' she taunted, despite being grateful for the cover.

'You can flaunt your skin in your own time. Right now you're operating on Heidecker time, and I'd rather not battle my way through frenzied paparazzi.'

He tucked the jacket closer around her and her gaze was drawn to the play of hard muscles under his expensive blue cotton shirt. Something tightened in her midriff and that damning tingle started once more. Hurriedly, she tore her gaze away.

She knew very well what her current predicament meant for Diamonds by Heidecker. The last thing she wanted to do was add to her list of sins by acknowledging her inexplicable feelings for its CEO.

He'd barely tolerated her when she was eight years old. That feeling had morphed into something else two months ago. It was something they'd never spoken of and both wished didn't exist between them.

Except it did…and they'd almost given in to it.

He looked down at her and she saw the reluctant gleam in his eyes. It was gone a second later. Pursing his lips, he captured her wrist and tugged her to the door.

The bolder paparazzi had already breached the outer limits of the courthouse. Years of practice had taught her never to look directly into the camera lenses—because somehow, no matter how much she tried, they always saw too much, revealed too much. Unfortunately, still feeling extremely unsettled, Ana now failed at what she'd practised since the age of seventeen.

The first flash blinded her. Heels meant for walking a few feet from car to dance floor gave way beneath her. Stifling a curse, Bastien caught her and swung her into his arms.

The world erupted in a blinding series of flashes and excited cries. With no choice but to ride the storm, she clasped her arms around his shoulders and buried her face in his neck.

His scent suffused her. Clean, musky…arousing. The warmth of his skin attacked her senses, throwing her back to that night on his yacht, when she'd let her emotions get the better of her. Her pulse quickened, her insides clenched tight as deep, illicit pleasure stole over her.

Ignoring the gossip-hungry media closing in on them, Bastien aimed straight for the black limousine with tinted windows idling on the pavement. One of the three burly men paving the way for them held the door open and they slid inside.

For several heartbeats neither of them moved. The door thudded shut. Silence cloaked them. The muted sound of the running engine hummed through her but still Ana didn't move. Her gaze skimmed the side of his face, unable to look away as she studied his arresting profile the way an artist studied his subject and committed it to memory.

The rocking of the car leaving the pavement caused her lips to graze the side of his neck.

Bastien exhaled sharply.

Her lids grew heavy as fierce sensation shot through her, radiating from her lips to spread over her body. The deep yearning to touch her mouth to his skin again became a surprisingly forceful rush of lust through her blood.

Abruptly Bastien leaned forward and deposited her on the seat opposite. With measured movements he secured her seatbelt before seeing to his own.

Ana felt the loss of his warmth as acutely as the loss of air in her lungs. She wanted to lift her fingers to her lips, press them against the tingling to keep it there for a moment longer, but Bastien had his laser gaze fixed on her, was watching her every move, waiting to pounce on any sign of weakness.

Fiercely she reminded herself that she wasn't weak…that she'd withstood worse. Growing up with a mother like hers had equipped her with a backbone that could endure most things.

So what if Bastien seemed to find his way under her armour with minimum effort? She wasn't about to cower under his formidable personality.

Gathering her composure, she cleared her throat. 'Thanks for helping me with the paparazzi—although I would've have handled it fine on my own.'

He sent her a stony look and settled back in his seat.

'Explain to me exactly what happened last night,' he commanded.

She raised her chin. 'Why? I'm sure you've seen the footage on the internet by now. One of your lawyers seemed ecstatic that it was trending on social media.'

One dark blond eyebrow lifted. 'That's all you have to say about the situation?'

'You won't believe me if I tell you, so what's the point?' she snapped, remembering his accusation in the courtroom.

He shrugged. 'We'll call this your second chance. You have my undivided attention, so let's hear it.'

'You've already decided what the truth is, Bastien. You said as much earlier when you referred to my "drug-fogged brain".'

'So you do remember that?' came his reply.

'Your mind's already made up, so why should I waste my breath?'

His smile mocked her. 'Because I want to hear what happened from the horse's mouth, so to speak.'

A spurt of anger speared through her. But alongside the anger came a small dart of hurt that he didn't believe her.

She contemplated silence, not dignifying his suspicions with an answer. But just as quickly she dismissed it. He was her boss. Her DBH contract had another month to run before she was finally free to join her father in Colombia. And a major condition of her contract stipulated her propriety and the maintenance thereof. The charges against her had put the DBH ad campaign at serious risk.

Bastien's presence in London—in court, in this car—made that fact painfully obvious.

He slowly straightened, leaned forward, and rested his hands on his knees without once taking his eyes off her. Ana knew she wouldn't get away without offering some kind of explanation.

She went with the simple truth. 'I suffer from asthma.'

He frowned, slate-grey eyes narrowing. 'I don't recall reading that in your personnel file.'

'You mean when you read it once you knew I was the one your management had hired for the campaign and tried to get me fired?'

It was the reason he'd been in Cannes that day. The reason he'd sent everyone away, leaving them alone on the yacht. The reason she'd ended up nearly losing her self-respect...

He didn't show an ounce of regret. 'Yes.'

She ignored the sharper dart of pain. 'Conditions that don't hamper the execution of my job aren't listed on my file, and asthma isn't generally a life-threatening illness. But I have it and I have to manage it, so...' She shrugged.

Lauren Styles, the owner of her agency, Visuals, and her own personal agent, had been aware of her condition and happy to keep it under wraps unless it hampered her job.

Lauren, once a model herself, was more of a mother to her than her own mother had ever been. Her loyalty and support were faultless. Which was another reason why she couldn't afford to jeopardise the DBH campaign or clash with its CEO.

'Go on.'

'My flatmate, Simone, invited me to her birthday party last night. I don't normally go to nightclubs because of the artificial smoke and recirculated air—I suffered a bad attack at a club last year. Halfway through the party I began to feel unwell.'

'Why didn't you just leave?' he demanded.

'I tried to. Simone begged me to stay.'

'Even though she knew you were ill?' Scepticism marred his tone.

'She doesn't know about my asthma.'

His brows lifted.

'We've only been sharing a flat for two months. Anyway, I

went into the cloakroom, splashed some water on my face, and used my inhaler when I got back to my table. I decided to stay for another half-hour. I went to the bar to get a bottle of water. When I returned to my seat the bouncers were waiting for me with the police. They showed me the security camera video, asked if it was me. I confirmed it was.'

Bastien pursed his lips.

'I didn't know then what it was all about, okay? They took me outside and asked to search my bag. They found the inhaler, charged me with possession of heroin and here we are.'

Silence cloaked the dark interior of the luxurious car. Outside, sunlight glinted off the buildings of Central London as they edged through the traffic on the Strand. Inside she was as cold as the January freeze they were experiencing. She pulled Bastien's jacket closer around her. For a few stolen seconds she let the scent of his body suffuse her senses. Then she looked up and found him watching…waiting.

'What? I've told you everything.'

He sat back, settled one ankle over his knee and drummed his fingers on the polished hand-stitched Italian leather. 'Not quite.'

Her gaze collided with his. Those compelling eyes held her prisoner, sending that familiar hot jolt she experienced every time she looked into those silver depths.

'I'm pretty sure I have.'

'I haven't heard you once deny drug possession.'

'Of *course* I've denied it. I've just told you what really happened.'

'You give me your version of events, but you haven't denied being a drug-user.'

She gasped. 'How dare you?'

He dropped his foot and surged forward until she could see every fleck in his eyes. 'Oh, I dare very much, Ana. You see, the welfare of my company is dependent on how *much* I dare. And so far, thanks to you, it's not doing so well.'

She straightened her spine. She'd done nothing wrong and she was damned if she would cower in fear. 'Fine. I don't use drugs. Never have—never will. Satisfied?'

His eyes narrowed. 'Did you leave your bag unattended at any point during the evening?' he fired back.

'I took it with me when I went to the bar but I may not have had hold of it the whole time. Look, I told the police all this.'

'But my interest in you is far more vested than theirs, so I think I deserve to hear your account, no?' His voice was soft, deadly.

Ana shivered. He was talking about his company, but she couldn't help but think back to that one very personal moment they'd shared on his boat. One that brought equal shame and excitement each time she relived it.

Brushing the feeling away, she glared at him. 'I get that—and, trust me, I want an explanation myself. Don't forget my reputation is on the line too.'

Not to mention the fact that she was in severe danger of being dropped from her father's volunteer programme if this situation got out of hand. Professor Santiago Duval might be a world-renowned archaeologist, but he'd drummed into his only child his hatred of favouritism.

Her father had despised that parasitic trait in her mother— the wife who'd fed on his prestige for as long as it suited her, then dragged him through a hellish divorce sixteen years ago. The wife who'd then eyed a Swiss banker, seen her way to a better life and selfishly grabbed at it, uncaring that she was wrecking lives.

She glanced at Bastien, wondered if he ever thought of that horrid winter. Or had he squashed it all beneath that icy demeanour?

'We are where we are. I assume you'll want to fire me from the DBH campaign again?' This time she didn't have much of a leg to stand on. But she intended to find a way to fight her charges and plead with her father to join his programme. Somehow.

His impassive look remained. 'As satisfying as that sounds, it's not that simple. The first adverts have already aired in the US and Japan. TV and media companies have been paid upfront for all three phases. Replacing you with another model now would mean shooting the whole thing all over again.'

'You want me to finish my contract?' She'd expected a swift, surgical exit from the Heidecker Corporation. 'But I thought…' She stopped when the in-car phone rang.

He answered it, his eyes staying locked on her. The incisive gaze made her aware of every sensitive pore on her skin, every breath she tried to take.

The tingling that had started in the courtroom flared again, rising to dangerous proportions as he conducted a leisurely survey of her body.

And through it all his features remained impassive.

Whoever had called and whatever news was being delivered reflected neither pleasure nor dissatisfaction his face. Bastien Heidecker had crafted his enigma into a fine instrument.

Even at fifteen, in the face of all the turmoil ripping their respective families apart, he'd never let his feelings show.

Except that one time…

He ended the call, replaced the handset and turned towards the window. Sunlight lit his features, turning his dark wavy blond hair a burnished gold. His strong, aquiline nose stood out in sharp relief and his clean-shaven jaw jutted out with uncompromising authority. His lips parted on a shallow breath, drawing her gaze to the exquisite shape of his mouth.

Ana held her own breath, willing him to keep looking outside. She told herself it was because she didn't want to resume their conversation, but she knew it was because she wanted to continue gazing at him—to take in the silky texture of his lashes as he lowered his eyelids and blinked…to remember what it had felt like to be kissed by those lips.

He turned suddenly and her heart flipped into her stomach.

'That was my CFO. DBH shares continue to tumble.' He glanced at his watch. 'And the market closes in thirty-five minutes.'

Apprehension knotted her stomach. 'What does that mean?' she asked around a dry throat.

His gaze hardened to tempered steel. 'It means you'd better start praying that the shares rally. Because if by close of play there's no sign of recovery then you, if we include the money I just stumped up for your bail, are liable to me for upwards of five million pounds.'

CHAPTER TWO

Shock ricocheted through Ana. 'I don't believe you.' The words spilled out before she could stop them.

His mouth compressed, and his eyes were as cold as the Alps of his native Switzerland.

Without answering, he pressed a button in the keypad near his wrist. She watched with escalating dread as a monitor sprang up from the centre console and flickered to life. Once it had clicked into place he angled it to face her.

The jumble of words and numbers scrolling beneath the picture on the screen sent a surge of almost debilitating insecurity rushing through her. Feeling his gaze on her, she struggled to remain calm, not to give him any more ammunition against her. But even without adequate understanding Ana had watched enough television to grasp what the graph meant. Heart thudding, she followed the red line descending with alarming speed.

At the top right hand corner of the screen she saw the time emblazoned clearly: 15:32.

'Turn it off,' she snapped hoarsely.

'That won't make it go away,' he rasped.

Pulling her gaze from the screen, she glanced down at her hands, saw the death grip she had on her purse and forced herself to relax. 'Turn it off, Bastien. You've made your point.'

The screen disappeared into its casing.

Nervously, she licked her lips. 'There must be something we...I can do?'

'*Not* being caught in possession of drugs would've been the single, most positive outcome to this whole situation.'

She glared at him. 'We can keep circling this conversation or we can discuss a useful way forward. Either way, my answer isn't going to change. I don't take drugs!'

'So you were framed? That's a little too convenient, don't you think?' he returned.

'*Convenient?* I've just spent the night freezing my behind off in a cold cell for something I didn't do. "Convenient" is the last way I'd describe my predicament.'

'Well, you'll have to start unravelling your predicament, fast. Your trial's in three weeks,' he informed her calmly.

'Three weeks?' Another wave of horror washed over her.

Bastien folded his arms over his chest. 'You expect me to believe you're not under the influence of drugs, and yet you can't recall events that happened less than an hour ago.'

'I was scared—all right?' Her voice emerged more shrilly than she'd intended.

A flash of emotion lit his eyes. She wanted to fool herself into thinking it was compassion, but it disappeared way too quickly for her to be certain.

She cleared her throat. 'I know I should've paid more attention in court. And I was. Before...before you showed up.'

'Are you saying I distracted you?'

'It wouldn't be the first time,' she replied.

His eyes narrowed but he didn't respond. Their time in Cannes was a subject they both wanted to avoid.

So why did she keep thinking about it...and reliving it?

No more.

She forced herself to look into his eyes.

'The last twelve hours have been difficult. I know it looks bad, but I haven't done anything wrong. Someone put the drugs in my bag. I don't know why. I'm innocent.'

She breathed a sigh of satisfaction when her voice stayed

even. She could do this. Remaining calm was key to finding a way out of this mess.

'Miss Duval, whether you're innocent or not, my company continues to haemorrhage money.' He flicked a glance at his watch. 'The market closes in twenty-five minutes. Someone needs to be held accountable.'

'But I can't do anything in twenty-five minutes!' Hysteria threatened to dissolve her shaky calm. Sucking in a desperate breath, she glanced out of the window.

And stiffened.

'This isn't the way to my flat.' Nor was it the way to the agency. The crazy thought that he was kidnapping her surfaced. Frowning, she brushed it away. Bastien had no reason to kidnap her. 'Where are you taking me?'

He took his time to brush away an invisible piece of lint from his neatly pressed trousers before resting his unsettling gaze on her. 'A condition of your bail was that I'd vouch for your whereabouts at all times. Which means that until your trial where I go, you go. I have to report to the board in Geneva first thing in the morning. You're coming with me.'

Ana's mouth dropped open for several stunned seconds before she snapped it shut. 'Like hell I am! Stop the car.'

She strained against her seatbelt, renewed trepidation rattling through her chest. She'd been in his company for less than an hour and already a feeling of panic far greater than she'd felt in court threatened her. After what had happened the last time she'd spent more than half an hour in his company, she didn't want to go a mile with Bastien Heidecker— never mind several hundred.

Why on earth hadn't she paid more attention in court? She would *never* have agreed to this condition.

Like you had a choice...

She silenced the taunting voice. There was always a choice, and she wasn't about to hand him her head on a plate. Furiously, she fumbled with the seatbelt, cursing silently when her numb fingers couldn't work it free.

'What do you think you're doing?' he asked, his tone mildly amused.

'Did you not hear what I said? I'm not going anywhere with you.' The belt snapped free. She lunged for the door. Thankfully, the car was cruising at a slow pace.

'And what? You intend to jump out of a moving car to avoid that?'

She grabbed the handle, her need to get out of Bastien's disturbing sphere of control paramount. 'Tell your driver to stop the car.'

Speculative eyes narrowed on her face. She was close to hysteria, but she didn't care. The need to escape was a living, writhing being inside her, demanding compliance.

'So you intend to flout the law and walk away from your responsibilities?' he asked, his voice a chilled knife.

'I intend to walk away from your bullying tactics. Don't think I don't know why you're doing this.'

'And why is it, exactly?'

Because of what happened in Cannes! Because of what my mother did to your family!

She swallowed the words. Voicing the details of their jagged past didn't seem like such a good idea.

'What good will taking me out of the country do? I'm much better off here, finding out what happened, don't you think?' she countered.

'I have no wish to be hauled to jail for breaking the law, Miss Duval. Besides, how are you going to find out who supposedly framed you?'

She bit her lip. 'I don't know yet.'

One eyebrow quirked. 'Let me know when you have a plan of action. In the meantime we follow the judge's ruling to the last letter.'

Despite his steady gaze and even steadier words Ana experienced a dark foreboding. Something dangerous lurked beneath his outward calm, warning her that once she took this step there would be no going back.

The thought seized her in its grip. 'No. I'm not going to hide from my situation, but neither am I going to Geneva with you.'

A look of cynical resignation crossed his face but he didn't speak.

The limo stopped at a traffic light. Without waiting for an answer, she yanked open the door.

For a split second she anticipated his icy voice ordering her to stay put, or—worse—the hands that had taken such domineering control of her at the courthouse hauling her back inside. But a heartbeat later she stood on the pavement, breathing in clear, fresh air.

Free.

Not stopping to examine the weird anti-climactic sensation enveloping her, she slammed the door and whirled away.

The icy January wind cut through her flimsy dress, its bite so ferocious it took her breath away. Clutching her purse in one hand, she pulled the lapels of the warm jacket around her. The sign for Charing Cross tube station beckoned. She started towards it. Only to stumble to a stop after a few steps.

As suddenly as it rose, her elation ebbed.

What was she doing?

'You intend to walk away from your responsibilities?'

Guilt gnawed at her. She'd done nothing wrong. She could repeat that to herself a thousand times over. Yet it didn't alter the reality of her situation.

Whether she liked it or not, she owed Bastien Heidecker. He might not have had grounds to fire her two months ago, but he had grounds now.

More importantly, he'd saved her from prison. He hadn't been obliged to bail her out or even to show up in court. But he had.

The memory of the fifteen-year-old Bastien who'd cleaned her cut when she'd fallen in his parents' garden in Verbier slammed into her thoughts. With crystal clarity she recalled his gentle hands as he'd tended her wound and the stoic but kind smile he'd bestowed on her once the plaster was in place. Even his admonishment to be careful on the loose steps leading to the garden had been gentle.

That had been the one and only time Bastien had genuinely smiled at her.

She pushed the memory away. There was an ocean of difference between that Bastien and this one. And even that Bastien had been an anomaly. It had been the only time during that whole miserable winter that he'd softened towards her. The rest of the time he'd frozen her out, looked right through her with those arctic grey eyes as if she didn't exist.

The urge now to pretend *he* didn't exist, to keep walking, was strong.

But she couldn't move. Her sense of integrity wouldn't allow her. Despite their chaotic past, he'd stuck his neck out for her.

And she'd never walked away from her responsibilities before.

She spun around. The lights had turned green and the limo was pulling into the traffic. Panicked, she raced after it, cursing as her heels nearly sent her flying again.

'Wait!'

Her shout was useless as the car sped away. Cold that had nothing to do with the freezing weather gripped her chest.

In the face of her mother's faithlessness Ana had tried to live her life by a strict moral code. And she'd just let herself down spectacularly.

Noticing the curious glances from passers-by, she swiped a hand over her face.

When the mobile phone rang she didn't recognise where it came from. Glancing down, she realised she still wore Bastien's jacket.

Frantically, she tore through the pockets, grabbed the phone and answered it.

'Have you come to your senses yet?'

* * *

Bastien watched Ana fight to control her irritation, the rise and fall of her chest rapid as she took several deep breaths. Against his will, his mouth twitched at the effort it took for her to remain silent. The child he'd known all those years ago wouldn't have held back her Latin temper at being made to chase after his car.

With her seatbelt on, her breasts stood out in proud prominence, the thin material of her dress displaying the tight peaks of her nipples. His senses stirred again, deeper, as he recalled how they felt, how they tasted. In her agitation earlier she'd bitten her lip repeatedly, making it fuller, redder than usual, making her natural, sensual pout even more pronounced, despite her mouth being pursed with displeasure.

He clamped down on the hot fizz of arousal and wrenched his gaze away. Unfortunately there was nowhere else on her body he could look without increasing the unwelcome sensations rampaging through him, threatening to drown him. Looking out of the window the way he'd tried earlier didn't work.

For reasons he couldn't comprehend his senses were sharply attuned to every move Ana Duval made. But this time he refused to succumb to the spell she was weaving.

He preferred curvy petite blondes with no baggage. He carried enough baggage from his childhood to last him a lifetime. And Ana Duval carried plenty of her own.

It was the reason he'd tried to have her thrown off his advertising campaign two months ago, when he'd discovered who his management team had chosen for the ads.

He'd been stunned when she'd actually smiled on seeing him on the boat. As if she was pleased to see him. When he'd made the reason for his visit clear she'd slowly, gracefully, uncurled herself from that sensual pose she'd been holding, faced him and dared him to do his worst.

And he nearly had...

Luckily he'd stopped himself in time—had walked away convinced that Ana, with her lithe, svelte figure and river of shining black hair, held no thrall for him.

Now he glanced into her wide, accusing eyes and willed the pounding in his blood away. He would never succumb to her temptation. Never be drawn into the emotional quagmire she carried with her. He was more than content living in his emotionally desolate state.

'You *knew* I was trying to stop the car and yet you pulled away.'

'I thought a few minutes in the cold would knock some sense into you.' Again, the urge to smile at her waspish tone pulled at him.

'You really are heartless—you know that?'

'What did you think? That I'd appear like a magical genie, rescue you from the big, bad judge and grant you three wishes into the bargain?'

The irritated flick of her head drew his attention to the sleek line of her throat, to the swift pulse hammering away under her smooth skin.

'No, of course not. But a little courtesy wouldn't have been amiss.'

'I'm not in the habit of granting courtesies to errant employees. Be grateful I didn't leave you to rot in prison.'

'Maybe you should have!'

The slightly hysterical edge to her tone gave him pause. With a tiny pang he admitted that perhaps he was being too harsh, letting his own frazzled state get in the way of clear thinking.

But then hadn't she had this effect on him last time?

'Does anyone hold a grudge against you and want to frame you like this?' he asked. The quicker they got to the bottom of her predicament the quicker they could go their separate ways.

The shadows receded from her eyes. Sharp sensation pierced him at her grateful look but he squashed it.

Her generous lips curved in a small, cynical smile. 'This is the modelling industry, Bastien. The number one rule is never to turn your back on a fellow model unless you want a knife buried in it.'

His name on her lips made that unnerving sensation pierce

harder. He shifted in his seat, his jaw clenching, and rejected the feeling. 'So you think someone's trying to jeopardise your position with DBH for their own ends?'

She shook her head, sending the silky tresses sliding over her shoulders. 'I don't see why. If someone wanted the assignment that badly they would've tried something at the beginning of the campaign—not when it's almost finished. How about you?'

Shock darted up his spine at her firm challenge. Witnessing her healthy suspicion made him want to laugh out loud. *'Excusez moi?'*

'Have *you* annoyed anyone lately? Anyone who'd want to see your business fail? I know I haven't done anything like that.'

'Nice trick to try and shift the blame on to me, Miss Duval, but no.'

She shrugged. 'It was worth a try. You're convinced I have skeletons in my closet. I merely wanted you to examine yours in case we were missing anything.'

'But I'm not the one charged with drug possession, am I?'

'Maybe a business rival is trying to get to you. What better way to bring down your company?'

He barely examined her line of reasoning before dismissing it. The last threatened takeover of one of the Heidecker companies had happened two years ago. He'd given the opposition a neat trouncing and sent them running with their tails between their legs.

'Another thing—we've known each other since we were children, so what's with the *Miss Duval*? Can't you call me Ana?' she suggested with a tentative smile.

The slight softening he'd allowed himself to feel immediately hardened.

How casually she'd tossed that memory into his lap. As if he hadn't spent years trying to forget that time—as if the repercussions of those horrific weeks they'd spent together hadn't lasted to this day.

Bitterness coated his mouth. 'We spent an unwelcome eight weeks together sixteen years ago—very much against our will—when your mother decided to seduce my father and he foolishly let his hormones get the better of him. You and I have crossed paths only once since that time. Do you need me to remind you of what happened then?'

She shook her head wildly but he ignored her.

'You flaunted your semi-nude body at me and I nearly ended up screwing your brains out. Tell me—do either of those scenarios qualify us as childhood friends?'

Her smile disappeared, along with a healthy dose of colour. Her fingers curled around each other, her knuckles white against her green dress.

'You're despicable!'

He felt no regret. From the success of the DBH campaign so far, and the meteoric rise in sales of the product, Bastien knew the power of Ana Duval's erotic thrall. Women wanted to be her. Men wanted to be *with* her. But she held no sway over him.

For her own sake he needed to make sure she knew that too.

'Will your flatmate be at home by now?'

Her head snapped up, her gaze hurt and wary. He looked away.

'She should be. Why?'

'You need a change of clothes. You'll be attending a board meeting with me in a little under sixteen hours. I recommend you do not do so dressed as you are right now.'

'What good will my presence there serve, exactly?'

He shrugged. 'By morning we'll know the extent of the damage to the company. Maybe your presence at the board meeting will be a precursor to your being fired and sued for damages.'

That hurt look returned and she bit her lip again.

Tearing his gaze away from her mouth was even harder, and the effort sent another dart of unease through him. Silence reigned in the car—one he didn't feel like breaking. His phone buzzed. He ignored it, curiously unwilling to hear any more news, good or bad, about what was happening outside the sphere he and Ana were in.

He watched her fumble through her bag, retrieve and activate her own phone.

How delicate her wrists were: frail, almost fragile, as if they were to be handled with the utmost care.

Bastien reeled back his wayward thoughts in time to hear her shallow gasp. Her colour receded even more as she listened to her messages.

Henry had already informed him after the meeting that the scandal involving the star of the DBH campaign had gone viral. Even the top international news stations were now leading with the story. Her voicemail would be crammed with every sleazy journalist wanting a piece of her.

Her clear distress grated.

'I suggest you turn off your phone and keep it turned off for the near future.'

For once she didn't protest. He watched one shaky finger press the power button. Then she went back to worrying at her lip with her perfect teeth.

Looking out of the window, she said woodenly, 'Will Simone get here before our flight's called?'

'We take off when I'm ready. Besides, your friend's not bringing your stuff here. I've sent someone to pick up the things you need. I didn't want her to be inconvenienced when my people turned up.'

Her head whipped round, a flash of anger widening her eyes. 'What if she hadn't been in?'

'Your landlady lives in the building. I'm sure she'd have accommodated my request.'

'You'd have gone through my possessions without my permission?' Incredulity rang through her husky voice.

'You owe my company a great deal of money, Miss Duval. I'd rethink any sense of misplaced anger, if I were you.'

'Well, you're *not* me! You might feel all high and mighty in that Heidecker tower in which you live, but normal people tend to treat each other with more respect.'

He glanced pointedly at the door. 'You're welcome to hop out again if you feel hard done by. But don't think for one minute that I won't come after you with everything I've got to make sure you honour our agreement.'

What little colour remained leached from her face. He watched her skim a shaky hand through her hair. The silky strands slid slowly through her fingers as she subsided into her seat. For several seconds she didn't speak, but her lips moved, formulating words with which to annihilate him. When she raised her eyes to his the chocolate-brown depths had darkened to almost black with the fierce fire burning within.

Raw, unfamiliar sensation gripped him, leaving a strong current rumbling along his nerves. The strange emotion made him feel disgruntled, made him shift in his seat. His eyes fell lower to her plump lips as they parted.

'I hate you.'

CHAPTER THREE

'HATE IS A very powerful word, *mi pequeña*. Never use it lightly.'

Her father's words echoed through Ana's mind as she glared at Bastien. Not since the age of nine, when she'd sobbed to her father after her mother had burned all of Ana's dolls in another bout of senseless cruelty had she felt that emotion so strongly.

But right now she hated Bastien Heidecker.

She hated the power he held over her—hated that he didn't feel an ounce of guilt at mercilessly wielding it. And hated that she had no recourse to fight him.

Despite taking control of her career the moment she'd turned twenty-one, Ana was still tied in to the six-year contract her mother had agreed with the agency just before she'd turned eighteen. Between their fees and her mother's extortionate managerial expenses she had very little financial capital to fight anything Bastien or his company might throw at her.

She was completely at his mercy and he knew it. He'd remained completely unruffled by her outburst, his unblinking gaze fixed on her.

'I can't afford that sum of money,' she added, just in case he'd missed her meaning before.

'You're a top model and a tabloid darling. I find it intriguing that you don't even have the money to bail yourself out of jail.'

'What I use my money for is none of your business. And surely you don't believe everything you read in the papers?'

His teeth bared in a mockery of a smile that made the hairs

twitch on her nape. 'I've learned, much to my regret, that there's almost never any smoke without fire. One way or the other, Miss Duval, you'll have to account to me at some point. Hate me all you like, but that's the reality.'

Without waiting for a reaction he flipped open his phone. The conversation flowed in rapid, flawless French. It carried on for almost fifteen minutes and the whole time Ana's heart pounded, the feeling of being completely immersed in her worst nightmare growing stronger by the minute.

In three weeks she had to return to court and fight drug possession charges. In the meantime she had to wait and see how the fall-out of this latest tabloid scandal would affect her. Not that she was a stranger to scandal. For as long as she could remember her mother had made sure to be caught in one on a regular basis—just to keep herself in the limelight. And if it happened to involve her supermodel daughter in some way, all the better.

Was it any wonder men like Bastien had the wrong idea about her?

Suddenly she yearned to speak to her father. To hear his calm, soothing voice. He was the one anchor she clung to when things got bad. But he was in the middle of the Amazonian jungle and their fortnightly phone call wasn't scheduled for several days.

'We're here.'

Bastien thrust the door open and stepped out. Blinking at the brilliant sunlight pouring in, Ana looked out onto a private airstrip.

She'd been so engrossed in the turbulent emotions Bastien aroused in her he might have driven her all the way to Outer Mongolia and she would have been none the wiser.

She glanced at the huge, gleaming jet sitting metres from the car and her heart sank. The Heidecker Corporation's blue and gold logo emblazoned on the tail brought home to her just how easily she could be crushed by the entity she'd taken on.

But then David had triumphed against Goliath…

She suppressed a bubble of hysteria and watched Bastien's strong, lengthy stride to the foot of the plane's steps, where his pilot waited.

She'd never wanted to fight with Bastien. From their first meeting sixteen years ago she'd tried to find friendly common ground with him, despite the dreadful irony of their circumstances. She'd tried myriad ways to prove that she wasn't his enemy, that they could be friends even as her mother was tearing his family apart. Deep down she'd known he'd resented her—not for her presence in his life, but because behind his chilly façade she'd been able to see the pain that echoed her own. She'd desperately wanted to reach him, to soothe away his pain in the hope that he would do the same for her.

How foolish she'd been...

She stepped out of the car and paused when another vehicle screeched to a halt beside her.

An excited Simone sprang from the vehicle and raced towards her.

'Oh, Ana, I'm so glad you're all right! When I heard what had happened I was horrified for you.'

Melodramatically she flung her arms around Ana. Two years younger than Ana, Simone Pascale had arrived in London six months ago from her native France and they'd ended up sharing a flat when Ana had accepted that living with her mother was no longer a viable option.

'And then these strange men turned up. At first I didn't know what to think. I mean, I was still super-excited for you and everything, because it's not, like, every day your flatmate leaves to shack up with a multi-billionaire—'

Ana pulled away. 'What? I'm not leaving to shack up with anyone. Whatever gave you *that* idea?'

Simone's over-bright blue eyes widened. 'But the pictures outside the court... And the paps were outside the flat, asking me if I knew how long you two had been a couple. I mean, *c'est très romantique, non*?'

Dread crept up Ana's spine. Glancing over her shoulder, she

saw Bastien watching her, eyes narrowed. 'Simone, what did you say to the reporters?' she whispered urgently.

'I said it was the best news ever and that I wished you much happiness… *Mon Dieu*, are you all right?'

Ana swallowed the sickening bile that had risen in her throat. She reached blindly to reassure Simone and felt her wrist being taken in a firm hold. Heat sizzled up her arm, electrifying her senses and reminding her of her weakness when it came to Bastien.

She pulled at her wrist. He held on tighter.

'What's going on here?' Steel underlined his voice.

'Nothing,' Ana interjected quickly, before Simone got a chance to spread her unwelcome news.

Bastien had barely tolerated being linked to her professionally. A romantic link would be even more abhorrent to him.

'I was just thanking Simone for helping me out.' Ana stared hard at Simone, who stood gaping at Bastien like a stunned fish.

'Do you have Miss Duval's passport?' Bastien asked her.

Rummaging through her bag, Simone located it and handed it over to him.

'*Merci*. That will be all.'

Ana glared at him for the pointed dismissal and turned to Simone. 'I'll give you a call later.'

Simone nodded and hugged her again. 'Hang on to him, Ana. He's absolutely *magnifique*!' she whispered feverishly.

'Let's go. I don't want us to miss our flight slot.' Bastien's impatient tone matched his stride across the tarmac.

She hurried up the steps, acutely aware of the shortness of her dress.

Once inside, she just stopped and gaped.

She'd flown in a few private planes with her job, but nothing had come close to the level of luxury accosting her senses now.

Royal blue carpeting stretched as far as the eye could see. Cream club chairs flanked both sides of the aircraft, separated by smooth marble tables on which stood exquisite flower displays and stylish lamps. The shades had been half pulled down over the windows to limit the glare of the late-afternoon sun and the atmosphere inside the craft was one of superb and seriously lavish comfort.

Ana would have been excited at being in such surroundings but for the darts of apprehension racing up and down her spine as once again the sensation of stepping into danger engulfed her.

A stewardess approached, a smile on her face as she greeted them and relieved her of Bastien's jacket. Weirdly, she felt exposed both inside and out without it. Pushing the feeling away, she murmured her thanks.

Bastien guided her into a chair and sat opposite her, his long legs stretched out on either side of her, imprisoning hers. She clamped her thighs together immediately, her senses screeching their awareness of him.

She thought of changing seats, then impatiently dismissed the idea. As long as he was close there would be no getting away from the discordant emotions bubbling underneath her skin. He'd always had that effect on her. Same as she knew she had an unsettling effect on *him*. Besides, she refused to let him intimidate her.

She glanced out of the window, feigning interest in the cargo trucks moving around a short distance away. But all too soon they were in the air, with clouds blocking her view of the landscape and taking away her reason for ignoring Bastien.

Steeling herself, she glanced at him.

He lounged in his chair, completely relaxed, eyes fixed on her, an unopened briefcase in front of him. Flushing, she wondered how long he'd been staring at her.

'Do I make you nervous?'

The laugh forced from her throat sounded false. 'Of course not. What gave you that idea?'

'You're skittish around me. I wonder why,' he said, almost conversationally.

'I'm not skittish—just annoyed that I'm tied to you for the next three weeks.'

'We all have a cross to bear, I suppose.'

She raised her chin. 'You're obviously as displeased about this as I am, so why did you vouch for me with the judge? Why not just elect one of your subordinates?'

'And make *them* liable should you decide to flee?'

'You have a very low opinion of me.' She didn't know why that hurt so much. 'Why is that, Bastien? What have I ever done to make you think so little of me?'

'I think we both know the answer to that.'

Her face flamed. 'What happened on the yacht—'

'You mean when you tried to use your body to change my mind about firing you?'

'That wasn't what I was doing…' She floundered and stopped as the memory tripped to life.

The moment she'd turned on the boat and seen Bastien standing on the deck, watching her, every nerve in her body had sprung to life.

The boy she'd known had grown into a breathtaking specimen of a man, with a commanding presence that had reached across the distance and held her captive. The smile she hadn't even been aware she'd given had slowly died as a deep, decadent awareness had arced between them. There'd been nothing boyish about the look in his eyes when he'd reached her.

'What are you doing here?' Fierce, flaying words—whispered through incredibly sensual lips.

It had taken her a minute to gather her senses. 'Hello to you too, Bastien.'

His mouth had compressed. 'Answer me.'

'I'm working—or at least I will be when you allow the crew to return. You've sent them away because…?' She turned away, because she couldn't look into those grey eyes without her midriff fluttering madly as if she was in the midst of a fever.

'You shouldn't have been given this commission.'

A lance of unsettling anger made her whirl about. He stood right behind her, so close her hair slid across his jaw. 'Why not? Because you still have a chip on your shoulder about our past?'

His nostrils flared. 'No. Because the brief called for someone conservative—not someone who...'

His deliberate pause, the drift of his eyes over her scantily clad body had sent flares of awareness and dark arousal all over her.

Her body's reaction shamed her, but she didn't give him the benefit of knowing he unsettled her.

Using her best catwalk pose, she planted her hands on her hips and cocked one hip. 'Someone who makes men want to drown their women in your diamonds? You don't want someone who makes wives, girlfriends and women who know what they want hit the speed dial for their nearest jeweller the moment the ads are aired? I'm sorry—I thought you were in this business to make money?'

Her smirk and her taunts were purely for self-preservation. The combination of magnetism, mild derision and lust she could see in his eyes deeply unsettled her.

As did his arctic smile.

'My vision for the product you're promoting isn't quite what you have in mind.'

'Really?' The tilt of her head had been well-practised for the camera. 'I read a survey recently. Next to pure silk, women voted diamonds as the sexiest thing to wear against their skin. So perhaps your vision needs to be a little less...*Victorian* and more sexy.'

He raised an eyebrow and slowly stalked her, not stopping until she was backed against the railing that overlooked the lower deck. Silence cloaked the upper deck, the rest of the crew having been dispatched somewhere below deck. Above them, stars glittered in the sultry evening. All around her Bastien's scent and imposing presence sent her heart-rate soaring.

'Are you telling me how to do my job, Miss Duval?' He caged her in, hands on either side of her, and treated her to narrow-eyed scrutiny.

'Just a little friendly advice. Sex sells—or haven't you heard.'

'And you're an expert in that field?'

She gasped, then tried to rein in her temper. 'I'm an expert at what I do. If you weren't sure who your target audience were perhaps you should've stuck to heading banks and building hotels.'

His icy imprecation rumbled along her nerves. 'You haven't stopped needing to play with fire, *ma petite.*'

'And *you* haven't stopped staring down your nose at me like I'm some inconvenience you can't wait to be rid of. Would it hurt you to be nice for once in your life?'

He froze. '*Nice?* Believe me, *cherie*, when I look at you, "nice" is the last thing I feel.' The words were whisper-soft but filled with a mixture of censure, need and puzzlement.

Her next question was inevitable—as was her need to draw even closer to that electrifying orbit. Before she could stop herself, she'd lifted her hand to his taut cheek, traced that stern jaw to the corner of his mouth. His sharp exhale made her shudder.

'What *do* you feel?'

'You don't want to know,' he muttered thickly.

'Maybe I do. Maybe for once I want to hear you vocalise what you actually feel, Bastien.'

He closed his eyes for a split second. *'Mon Dieu...'*

She rose on tiptoe and pressed her lips to his, the need a wild clamour that wouldn't be stopped. His hands clamped on her immediately. One at her waist, the other in her hair. He held her prisoner and deepened the kiss, his groan a rough, hungry sound. He branded her with his mouth and his hands and she willingly gave him complete access.

It might have been seconds or minutes later that she found herself on her back on a lounger, his head between her bared breasts, her swimsuit bunched somewhere around her waist. Her hoarse cry when his fingers slid beneath her suit to tease her wet heat made him raise his head. His eyes were molten with intense need.

'You want to know how I feel? Right now I want to take you, possess you, make you forget every other man who has come before me.'

'Why?'

'Because you've been under my skin since the first time I saw you. A precocious kid who wouldn't take no for an answer. You watched me with those soulful eyes and dogged my every step until I couldn't move without you tripping me up. You're *still* under my skin. Everywhere I look you're on a billboard or on the side of a bus. Except now you make me ache—make me crave things I do not want to crave.'

'And you hate me for that?'

His smile made her breath catch.

'I hate that you have a certain…power over me. I cannot allow that.' His fingers moved and his mouth closed over her nipple.

She shuddered as his imposing erection pressed deeper into her belly. 'So…what? You're going to use your position to bring me to heel? Or are you going to use sex?'

A part of her couldn't deny the thought excited her, but another part recoiled from the idea.

He froze and locked eyes with her. A frown slowly creased his brow, then his gaze drifted over her semi-nude body. He swallowed and shook his head, as if divesting himself from the clutches of a bad dream.

He started to rise but she locked her fingers behind his head.

'Bastien…' She wasn't sure what she wanted to say but she hated the look in his eyes.

He firmly disentangled himself from her and stood. 'I'm ashamed to admit that was my intention.' He shoved a hand through his hair. 'What did you say—sex sells? How very right you are.'

The delivery was cold. And although most of the censure in his voice was directed at himself, a healthy dose spilled her way.

Rushing to rise and right her clothes, she felt fury cut through her lust haze. 'You can't fire me for doing my job, Bastien!'

He turned away, as if he couldn't bear to look at her. 'No, but I *will* keep a close eye on you from now on.'

'Go ahead. And be sure to send me a thank-you bonus when your sales go through the roof.' Burning at the thought of that day, Ana glared at Bastien. 'So things got out of hand before we could stop ourselves? That's what you get for being so vile!'

He stared back for several seconds, then shrugged. 'Let's blame my unexpected discovery of just who it was my marketing people had chosen for my campaign.'

She frowned. 'You mean you didn't know?'

'I'm not in the habit of micromanaging my businesses. You, on the other hand, *knew* who you would be working for. Why did you take the assignment?'

'Because I foolishly hoped the past could remain in the past.' She locked eyes with him, saw the stormy emotions swirling in his grey eyes. 'Surely you can't blame *me* for what happened sixteen years ago?'

She hated herself for caring enough to want to know, but the idea that they would be locked in that volatile winter for ever made her heart lurch sickeningly.

For several seconds he said nothing. Then, 'No, but it doesn't make the reminder of that time any less palatable.'

His response dashed the tiny burgeoning hope she'd harboured.

'So you're saying you'll never look at me and not remember what happened then?'

'*Non.*'

An icy numbness settled over her. 'Well, I guess that's definitive enough. Oh, and for what it's worth, I never set out to use my body to convince you to let me keep my job. What happened...just happened.'

'A lot of things "just happen" with you around, I'm discovering.'

Anger washed away the numbness. 'Oh, screw you, Bastien,' she flung at him, then flushed from head to toe at her unfortunate choice of words.

He laughed—the sound as unexpected as it was pleasing. She gave in to a reluctant smile and breathed easier.

* * *

'I asked for your suitcase to be delivered to the cabin. Perhaps you'd like to change once we reach cruising altitude?' he suggested, bringing her back to the present.

His consideration made her soften. Nodding, she relaxed her taut muscles a fraction—only to tense again as her bare leg rubbed against his calf. Heat dragged low in her belly and a familiar tingling shot to the apex of her thighs.

Clamping her legs tightly together, she muttered, 'Thank you.' The quicker she was out of his presence, out of this dress and back in the comfort of jeans and a top, the better she'd feel.

Grabbing a magazine from the nearby stack, she flipped blindly through the glossy pages.

'There's also a shower if you wish to make use of it.'

She froze, refusing to think of Bastien naked, wet or otherwise. But a persistent image took root, imprinted itself on her brain and sent her heart-rate soaring.

His added, 'It's not large, but it'll do,' caused her hand to tremble so badly she dropped the magazine.

What on earth was wrong with her?

She darted a glance at him to see if he'd witnessed her discomfort. His nostrils were pinched, his jaw clenched, his eyes a shade that reminded her of how he looked when he was aroused.

She tried to look away. His gaze held her prisoner. Images of him underneath a shower, naked, flooded her mind. Ripples of desire surged through her abdomen, radiated outwards until her limbs felt weak, leaden.

Slowly his eyes swirled with heat, like the smoke from a rumbling volcano just before it erupted. She didn't have much experience when it came to men, but an unavoidable by-product of her profession was learning very quickly to interpret lust.

Bastien's eyes reflected a danger that would consume her given half a chance. Her breath locked; that secret, swollen place between her legs throbbed harder.

His gaze dropped to her exposed thighs and lingered for endless seconds, and his Adam's apple bobbed as he swallowed.

Heat continued to drag through her. Unable to stay still, she slowly crossed her legs.

Bastien followed the movement, his eyes roving over her until she wanted to scream…scream something at him.

The loud 'ding' signalling the seatbelts sign being turned off jerked her out of the dangerous quicksand. A moment later the stewardess pushed back the curtain and stepped into the cabin.

Dazed, Ana watched Bastien's eyelids sweep down, veil his expression. Pressing a button in the wall, he pulled out a laptop and slid it open.

She envied his steely control, wished she could harvest a tiny fraction of it and not feel as if the maelstrom of sensations buffeting her body would rip her in two.

The stewardess set down a tray of drinks. Before she could serve them, Bastien said, 'Mathilde, please show Miss Duval to the bedroom.' His voice too was smooth as silk.

'Of course.'

'We'll eat when you return,' he said, without looking up from his papers.

Ana struggled to her feet, irritated and more than a little bit confused.

The last thing she needed was to develop any feelings for Bastien. But for the life of her she couldn't seem to draw on the composed, unruffled demeanour she usually projected for the camera.

The thought scared her more than she cared to admit. Was Bastien right? Would they never be able to be in each other's presence without the past rearing its dangerous head? And would this insane attraction eventually whizz itself out of control? Or would it grow stronger, like a tornado, devouring everything in its path?

She summoned a smile when Mathilde indicated the cabin door to her left.

In a large mahogany-panelled bedroom, Ana found herself alone for the first time since being taken from her cell that morning. She froze when she realised she hadn't even thought of her predicament for the last hour.

Her hands trembled as she grappled with the realisation that Bastien, despite his high-handed and autocratic attitude, made her feel...*safe*.

It was the same feeling that had compelled her to continually seek him out at his parents' house sixteen years ago—had made her ignore his *keep out* demeanour.

Never mind the excitement bubbling underneath her skin, the heat scouring her abdomen in that dangerous, delicious manner whenever she was close to him, her underlying feeling with Bastien was that he would never deliberately hurt her.

Which was completely irrational, of course.

Hoping that time away from his unsettling presence would restore her equilibrium. along with her common sense, she shed the offensive silk dress and entered the bathroom.

What it lacked in space it made up for in opulence and accessories. Cosmetics designed for both sexes adorned the shelf space. For a charged, insane moment her mind conjured up Bastien sharing this bedroom with a lover, showering with her in this bathroom.

With a hiss of impatience she stripped off her panties and stepped beneath the warm spray. What Bastien did with his lovers was nothing to do with her.

Soaping her body, she washed quickly, resolutely refusing to think about the man who could flip her world upside down with minimal effort and thinking instead of who had gone to such lengths to frame her.

For a wild moment Ana wondered if her mother had been behind the frame-up. But that didn't make sense. Lily Duval would never mess with the source of her income. Getting Ana thrown off the DBH campaign would attract the sort of scandal her mother craved, but even *she* wouldn't bite the hand that fed her.

Which meant there were no other suspects in the frame.

Sighing, Ana turned off the shower and grabbed a towel. Padding to the bedroom, she unzipped her suitcase...

And flicked through the packed clothes with growing horror.

The jeans, cotton tops and wool-blend sweaters she'd expected were nowhere in sight. Instead she pulled out the skimpy outfits from her last fashion show, saucy lingerie from a recent underwear shoot and silk, lace, sheer chiffon see-through wisps of nothing that made up the theme of this year's spring/summer collection.

Sinking onto the bed, Ana crushed a silk bra in her fist.

It didn't take a genius to work out that Simone, believing Ana was embarking on a torrid love affair, had packed clothes fit for a woman out to drive her lover crazy with lust.

She choked off a feverish bubble of laughter and dug through her case with renewed vigour, a cry of relief escaping when she grasped what felt like denim.

Pulling it out, her spirits sank lower. The material of the jeans was slashed in so many suggestive places it was downright indecent. She'd modelled them two weeks ago, on a shoot for an up-and-coming designer. Once on, they would cling like a second skin, the stretchy material revealing even more flesh.

Another frenzied search produced a soft cashmere sweater. The batwing design covered her arms, although it left her with an exposed cleavage and back, and its dramatic style made wearing a bra nonsensical. Not great, but at least it covered her midriff.

Curbing a growl of frustration, she passed a brush through her hair, trying not to look into the floor-length mirror next to the bathroom door as she did so.

She gathered her hair on top of her head and pinned it in place. Bastien already thought she used her body to achieve her own ends. His opinion of her couldn't sink any lower. Besides, she'd endured worse looks from men in the past.

But none of them made your pulse hammer so hard, or made you aware of every erratic breath you took.

Pursing her lips, she grasped the door handle and opened it.

Bastien's huge frame filled the doorway.

'Are you stalking me?' she snapped.

His mouth quirked. 'I was beginning to wonder whether you'd launched yourself out of the nearest air lock.' His penetrating gaze captured hers and something throbbed to life in her chest.

'The idea was tempting, but the thought of food won against the need to escape.' Her stomach rumbled in agreement and she grimaced.

'Then by all means come, let's satisfy your hunger…' he drawled mockingly—then froze, his gaze fixed over her shoulder.

Cringing, Ana glanced back at the clothes strewn on the bed.

She rushed to the bed and lunged for the clothes. Only to stop when his suppressed hiss made her head jerk around. His eyes were riveted on her behind, his laser gaze burning right through the wide slash in the jeans exposing half her bottom.

'When I suggested presentable clothes, this wasn't what I had in mind,' he rapped out, his face taut with more than a hint of wild hunger.

Roiling emotions jerked through her. 'This wasn't what I had in mind, either. But that's what you get for not giving me a chance to pack my own clothes.'

Crossing his arms over his chest, he rested one muscled shoulder against the doorjamb. 'So this is *my* fault? Don't get me wrong—I'm not complaining at the view. Merely thinking that January in Geneva isn't the time to be exposing acres of flesh, delectable though it might be.'

'Well, until I can buy myself a coat you'll just have to avert your eyes. Or is that *really* the problem?' she challenged, then kicked herself at poking the dragon.

'I assure you, controlling my baser urges has never been my problem, Miss Duval. Right now you're more in danger of contracting pneumonia than attracting my attention.'

'Watch it, Bastien, you're being vile again,' she snapped.

He shoved a hand through his hair, ruffling the smooth blond waves. 'You drive me to it.' He stopped and breathed deep. 'If you want to eat, come now. The food's getting cold.'

Tight-jawed, he stepped aside and waited for her to precede him.

Ana suppressed the impulse to refuse food, slid past him and hurried to her seat, keenly aware of his merciless scrutiny as he followed.

She polished off Caesar salad and a basket of warm French bread in record time, then sat back in her seat.

Exhaustion had sapped her strength. Their verbal wrangling on top of everything that had happened in the last twenty-four hours was taking its toll. The warm shower had helped, but weariness still tugged relentlessly at her muscles.

When he moved away and opened his laptop again after their meal she breathed a sigh of relief and retreated to the farthest club chair, trying to formulate a plan of action on how to defend herself against her charges.

Within minutes she'd given up, her concentration having fractured every time she came within touching distance of a coherent thought. Instead her brain remained locked on the look on Bastien's face when she'd turned around in the bedroom. The naked hunger that had burned in his slate-grey eyes replayed itself over and over in her mind until breathing became difficult.

Desperate to escape the cloying atmosphere, she almost applauded when the stewardess announced that they were landing in fifteen minutes.

The plane had barely taxied to a halt when Bastien looked up and issued a command in French to the stewardess. She retreated to the back of the aircraft and returned with a long, faux-fur-lined coat, which she handed to Ana.

It was only after she'd gratefully shrugged into the warm coat that a distasteful thought occurred to Ana.

'Who does this coat belong to?' she asked past the inexplicably jarring thought that it might belong to someone he'd been with, perhaps even touched with the same hunger he'd touched her with on his boat.

The sensation was so strong that she was halfway to tearing off the garment when his voice stopped her.

'Mathilde keeps a selection of clothes to accommodate the different temperatures around the world. I suggest you wipe that sour look off your face and show some gratitude,' he mocked.

Heat suffused Ana's face. 'I'm sorry…'

He waved her away. 'Save it, Miss Duval. You can't help who you are.'

Without waiting for the pilot Bastien reached past her, pulled down the handle and thrust open the heavy plane door. Cold air rushed into the cabin, accelerating the freeze seizing her insides.

She rushed after him. 'What's that supposed to mean?'

He turned and immediately the cold receded. She felt hot, stung alive by the heated censure blazing from his eyes.

'You breathe your sexuality. I offered the use of my shower and immediately you thought of us, wet, sharing that confined space. When I came to the bedroom door your pulse thundered, and if I were a betting man I'd wager that you couldn't keep thoughts of us in my bed out of your mind. Even sharing a meal with me just now got you so hot and bothered you couldn't formulate a civilised conversation. Feel free to correct me if I'm wrong.'

She gasped. 'Yes! No! That's totally out of— I dare you to tell me you weren't thinking those same thoughts!'

Surprise preceded a flare of heat across his cheekbones. Then he shrugged. 'Perhaps. But I'm better at compartmentalising my emotions than you are. I don't rush to assumptions.'

'Oh, really? You've rushed to find me guilty of everything so far.'

'Because I can't ignore the evidence. To overlook it would be extremely naïve. And that is one thing I'm not.'

Her fingers clutched the lapels of her borrowed coat at her throat, as if she would keep his sharp words out. 'Of course not. You're above reproach, above temptation, unlike the rest of us mere mortals. But you know what suppressing your feelings does to you eventually? It deadens you inside.'

His brow quirked in silent mockery. 'You think I'm dead inside?'

He seized one of her hands and laid it flat against his chest.

His heart beat heavy and steady beneath her palm before he drew it slowly down, past his belt, to the thick evidence of his manhood.

'I don't think you want a reminder of how quickly I can refute that statement, *cherie*.'

She heard movement behind her and wrenched her hand free as the pilot and Mathilde approached. Bastien grasped her arm and propelled her down the short steps.

Ana forced one foot in front of the other, reeling from Bastien's words as they approached a black Bentley waiting on the tarmac.

'Our last encounter confirmed to me that you're an intensely sexual creature, Miss Duval, with impulses that define who you are,' he whispered into her ear.

The sound of her name on his lips, spoken with that sexy French lilt, caused her stomach to flip in the most alarming way, making her miss the actual words he'd uttered.

'Don't presume that you and I are the same.'

Anger finally loosened her tongue. 'That's great—because I wouldn't wish to be anything like you if you paid me a billion dollars.' Snatching her arm away, she stalked to the car and slid into the seat.

He followed, and for the second time that day she found herself enclosed in the back of a luxury car with Bastien Heidecker. Only this time they weren't on opposite sides. This time he slid in next to her, his thigh coming to rest so dangerously close to hers that heat from his body surrounded her like a force field.

He started to reach for his seatbelt and her eyes dropped to the hard expanse of his chest underneath the fitted cotton shirt. She glanced up quickly and met his mocking gaze. Traitorously, another wave of heat crawled up her face.

'Save the act, Miss Duval. Pretending outrage while your eyes devour me wears thin after a while,' he sliced at her.

'God, you *are* full of yourself, aren't you? The outrage is real. I've never met anyone more infuriating than you. And there's nothing remotely sexual about that!'

She was so intent on congratulating herself with her come-back she didn't acknowledge the charged silence until his hand landed on her shoulder.

'Then this shouldn't affect you too much.'

'Wha—?'

His lips slanted over hers before the word could come out. Ana's world imploded.

Every coherent thought, every ounce of outrage, fled as she experienced Bastien—up close and devastatingly personal.

His kiss started out as a ruthless lesson and very quickly became something else. Something that made her stomach muscles quiver.

His lips, hot and urgent, branded hers, evoking such electrifying reactions she could do nothing but cling on, open herself to the pleasure drenching her.

Never had she been kissed like this. Never had need pummelled her so relentlessly. The fist she aimed at his chest unfurled and slid over warm corded muscles to band around his neck. Thick, luxurious hair caressed her fingertips and she explored the strands, experiencing a whole new sensual feast as she moulded his scalp in her hands. She would never have imagined hair could be this sensual to touch…? Who was she kidding? Everything with Bastien held an extra-special edge that threatened to floor her.

Bastien had called her reaction to him an act. Except it wasn't an act. The world might think Ana Duval represented sex on legs, but the truth would shock them even more. The fact was that she was as far removed from being sexually promiscuous as was humanly possible.

'You are an intensely sexual creature…'

No!

So why was she almost prone in the back of a car, with a bristling alpha male who made her panties damp with desire and her pulse hammer as his hot mouth kissed its way down her exposed cleavage?

Ice drenched her, stiffened her body and lent her the strength to push at Bastien's shoulders. Even so, she couldn't help a smothered groan when his lips grazed one tight, cashmere-covered nipple. The absence of a bra meant his touch manifested itself much more brazenly, its thrilling effect nearly sending her into orbit. Heat shot from her nipple to her clitoris, drenching her in even more shame.

'Stop!'

Her frantic cry got through to him. The hands curled possessively around her waist stilled. In the darkness of the car he raised his head and speared her with gunmetal eyes. The hungry blaze in their depths made her quake. His gaze fell to her lips. As if he'd kissed them again they tingled and swelled.

Slowly he rose and settled back into his seat.

Ana struggled up and straightened her clothes. Minutes ticked by. He said nothing—just continued to stare at her.

Trying desperately to hide her flustered state, she fixed her hair and finally faced him. She tried not to think of how his fingers, now clenched into a fist on his thigh, had trailed fire on her skin, how quickly and devastatingly they'd evoked raw, turbulent feelings inside her.

Resolute, she cleared her throat. 'If you were trying to prove a point with that…that display, I should warn you it proved nothing.'

His face remained impassive. 'That you feel the need to caution me speaks for itself.'

'Well, I'd appreciate it if you didn't pounce on me without warning like that in future.'

His low laugh infused the dark interior of the car with rich sound. 'You think a gold-embossed request next time is going to make this insane chemistry between us more benign?'

'I'd prefer it if you didn't touch me at all.' She pulled the coat tighter around her, chilled despite the warmth of the car.

Once again she'd let Bastien shake the foundations of her painfully constructed fortress of self-control and allowed her emotions to get the better of her.

How many times had she seen her mother succumb to the

emptiness of lust and need, only to be left high and dry and even more embittered? And how many times had she borne the brunt of her mother's misery? She couldn't, *wouldn't* give in to whatever deceptive, tumultuous sensations Bastien elicited from her.

She was in control of her life, of her feelings. And she aimed for it to stay that way.

'Promise me it won't happen again.' The slight edge to her tone made her suck in a breath and battle to remain calm.

For several seconds he remained silent. Then he hooked a finger under her chin.

Bastien had watched her struggle to bring herself under control and felt a strange kinship with her as he battled his own raging libido. Things had got out of hand far too quickly.

He knew the full cost of giving one's emotions free rein. He'd watched his mother wear her heart on her sleeve every day—only to have it exploited, twisted and broken apart until only a shell remained. A shell that had had no use for a son's presence, never mind his love.

His aim since that bleak winter had been to protect himself against that feeling at all costs. And he'd succeeded…for the most part. Until Ana.

His gaze dropped to her still-damp lips—lips that had tasted much sweeter than he'd remembered from that one other time when he'd lost control and let her slip beneath his guard. The day he'd almost stripped her naked on the deck of his yacht.

His groin hardened all over again as he recalled the smooth valley between her breasts, now fully covered with the wide lapels of a coat two sizes too big. His mouth had grazed the hard nub of her nipple only briefly, but the imprint remained vivid, branded on his lips.

With a swallowed groan he dropped his hand, willed his control back, and cast around wildly for a subject to kill the desire swirling inside him.

'How's your mother these days?'

In the dim light her eyes widened warily at the change of subject before she glanced down at her hands. He knew very well that he hadn't answered her question, or given her the promise she sought. He had no intention of doing so.

Ana Duval had no right to seek promises from him. Certainly not ones he wasn't entirely sure he could keep. She unsettled him far too much, emotionally and physically, for him to be anywhere near certain about any damned thing.

When she looked up her anxious expression was gone, replaced by an icy hauteur that was meant to freeze him out. He almost laughed.

'She's fine—but somehow I think you know that.'

She wasn't wrong. Lily Duval's thirst for the limelight made her impossible to ignore.

'Since we're being polite, how's your father?' she returned, her tone conversational, as if she'd bounced back from the passionate storm that had so nearly ravaged them.

But the wild pulse beating at her throat betrayed her. He prided himself on his control, and even he hadn't brought his body to heel yet.

'My father retired seven years ago. He and my mother live in Gstaad for most of the year now.'

His father was living with his guilt from sixteen years ago. Away from the shame he'd brought to his family and the chaos his actions had caused the company.

'Do you see them often?' she asked in a low, tentative voice.

He shrugged and answered despite the unsettling ache thinking about his parents brought. 'I make a trip when my father insists on seeing me.'

'When was the last time?'

The ache intensified. 'Three weeks ago.'

As usual his mother had barely known who he was, stoked up by the drugs prescribed for her condition. When his father had tried to prompt her memory he'd only succeeded in agitating her further. The visit had gone downhill very fast and Bastien had left, ignoring his father's pleas to stay.

'I'm glad they're still together,' she ventured, a wary little smile teasing her lips. 'Your father was nice to me.'

'*Oui,* he's always had a weakness for a pretty face.'

She flinched, and mingled regret and bitterness bit deep, finally eradicating the last of his unwanted desire. Whereas he'd have smothered the emotions before, this time he gave them space. He needed to remind himself why control over his emotions was imperative. Why the erratic feelings between Ana and him risked pulling away the rivets he'd fastened over his emotions.

Because even as an angelic eight-year-old Ana had charmed and entranced everyone around her—including his father. He remembered his father's encouragement for Bastien to get to know sweet Ana—'She'll be your sister one day, you know.'

The last thing he'd felt towards her then was brotherly, because every time he'd looked at her he'd been reminded that he was witnessing his family's destruction.

And the woman who sat next to him now, with her smooth legs crossed in the most alluring of ways, her eyelids lowered over chocolate-brown eyes as if keeping seductive secrets from a lover, engendered no brotherly feelings whatsoever inside him. A handful of minutes ago her body, warm and tempting, had surged against his, and her breath had come in passionate pants as she'd lost herself in her pleasure.

Mon Dieu, brotherly was the last thing he'd ever feel towards her.

He clenched his fingers against the urge to grab her chin again and make her look at him; to kiss her again and smother the bitterness of the past and the hunger of the present. He took a deep breath instead, reasserted control and reminded himself of one thing.

Regardless of their past, Ana Duval was as guilty as hell of the chaos now rippling through his life right now. She'd tested his control two months ago and she continued to test the edge of his resolve, reminding him of the vulnerability of emotion.

And *that* he would not forgive.

CHAPTER FOUR

ANA TOOK ONE last look at her image and brushed a hand over her dark grey suit jacket. Its precise, severe style suited her purpose. With her hair caught and pinned up out of the way, she projected a professional image—one that was far removed from the image the paparazzi had plastered all over the internet in the last twenty four hours.

Although the cost of the Armani skirt suit, chosen hurriedly from the hotel's boutique last night, would put a serious dent in her finances, she'd had no choice. Facing Bastien's board members wearing anything from her suitcase wasn't an option.

A knock signalled the arrival of breakfast, although eating was the last thing she felt like doing.

Bastien's taut silence after that incident in the car last night gave her little hope that he'd be any different today. He'd closed down, shutting her out as effectively as he'd done at fifteen.

On arrival at their luxurious hotel he'd left her outside her suite with an order to be ready at nine. But sleep had been elusive, and her long, restless night had been spent reliving that kiss and how she would survive the next three weeks in the emotional cauldron that was being around Bastien.

Another knock fractured her thoughts. She let the waiter in and he wheeled a trolley underneath the window facing a picturesque view of Lake Geneva.

In the early-morning light the Alps and Mont Blanc rose majestically in the distance, the rolling range curving almost protectively around the city. She'd travelled to other parts of Switzerland on photo shoots but had never visited its best-known city.

Ana sat down at the table…forced herself to eat two pieces of buttered toast and a mouthful of scrambled eggs. It was just as she lifted the glass of orange juice that she spotted it.

A newspaper was tucked underneath the napkin, and on its front page was her picture. Only it wasn't just her picture. The photo showed her in Bastien's arms, emerging from the court yesterday. Showed the way she'd clung to him like a limpet, her eyes closed and her face buried in his neck as if…as if he was her protector.

God…

But that wasn't the worst of it. It was the look on Bastien's face that made her hands shake as she unfolded the paper.

What she could understand of the caption froze her blood.

Heidecker's New Love. Is He the Cure for this Drug-Addicted Supermodel?

Skimming the article, she desperately tried to recognise enough words to understand what the article said. Her horror grew as she spotted Simone's name repeatedly. Her breakfast surged upwards, making a bid for freedom.

She barely made it to the bathroom before she emptied her stomach's contents. Trembling from head to toe, she wrenched at the tap, rinsed her mouth, then clutched the sink, eyes squeezed shut, struggling to breathe.

This was the absolute last thing she needed…

Standing there, propped against the sink, she didn't realise the pounding wasn't just in her head until she heard her name called out.

'Open the door, Miss Duval.'

Heart leaping into her throat, she prised her fingers from the cold porcelain and approached the bathroom door.

She cracked it open. 'What do you want, Bastien?'

He surged into the room. 'What took you so long?'

A few smart answers rose to her lips but she smothered the more hysterical ones when she caught his frown. 'What...?'

'You look pale. Are you all right?' He laid a hand against her forehead.

For several seconds she couldn't speak. 'I'm fine,' she finally managed. 'How did you get in here?'

'This hotel belongs to me.' He dropped his hand. 'HH Geneva is one of several hotels owned by my bank.'

The HH Group—Heidecker Hotels—was renowned for its understated opulence, was yet another feather in the Heidecker cap...a fact she'd missed with her weariness last night.

'It doesn't explain what you're doing in my room,' she replied, cringing as she wondered whether he'd heard her retching.

'I told you to be ready at nine—that was five minutes ago. When you didn't answer your door I let myself in. Don't fret. If I'd hoped to catch you naked I'd have turned up an hour ago as you took your shower.'

'Careful, there, Bastien, or I'll add Peeping Tom to your list of unsavoury characteristics.'

That earned her a mocking look as he returned to the sitting room and crossed to the open suite door. He didn't slam it. Yet the decisive snick of the lock and a glimpse of what he held in his fist sent a shaft of pure, unadulterated dread through her.

He unfurled another newspaper. The front-page picture was the same as on hers, but the language was different.

'Tell me what you know about this,' he invited softly.

'If you're asking if I've seen the paper, yes—I have.' Her eyes inadvertently slid to the breakfast table. Her heart sank as he followed her movement.

The temperature in the room dropped another degree. 'Of course you have. Did you salivate over it before or after you had your breakfast?'

'Excuse me?'

He ignored her outrage. 'How much are the tabloids paying you for this?'

'What? You're insane if you think I had something to do with this!'

'So you deny you had anything to do with this rubbish?'

'Absolutely I do,' she stressed.

'Then tell me what you were hatching with your flatmate on the tarmac yesterday.'

Ana's mouth dropped open. No words emerged and she knew her guilt was stamped on her forehead. Belatedly, she tried damage limitation. 'Seriously, it was nothing like that—'

'Do you take me for a fool?'

'Only if you believe everything you read in the paper!' The volatility of her words hit home the moment they left her lips. She surged on, regardless. 'Bastien, think about this. What could I possibly have to gain by pulling this stunt?'

He crumpled the paper and tossed it down on the nearby coffee table. It missed and landed on the floor.

Slowly, with the precision of an Alpine wolf on a blood trail, he stalked her until he stood so close she could see the pulse leaping in his temple, smell the mixture of fury and his unique masculine scent.

Nothing promised an upside to this situation.

'Right now you need someone to fight your corner. Who better than the CEO of the company that's about to turf you out on your ass?'

She stared back, unable to look away from the hypnotic intensity of his eyes. 'So you've decided, then?'

'After this stunt I'd be a fool not to cut you loose,' he replied.

'Believe what you will. I had nothing to do with this article, whatever it says.'

His eyes narrowed. 'You're now pretending you don't *know* its contents?'

Realising what she'd almost let slip, she pursed her lips. Besides her father, who'd been horrified when she'd finally confessed her secret and immediately fought to make things right, and her mother, who'd been the cause of it, no one else knew.

'I stopped reading any stuff written about me a long time

ago.' The lie made her cringe, but it was way better than the shameful truth. 'Maybe if you tell me which part so concerns you I can address it.'

Bastien's brows slowly lifted, incredulity darkening his eyes to gunmetal. 'Which part so concerns me? Let's see— how about the part that suggests we've been lovers for the best part of six months? No, actually, that doesn't concern me too much—although it suggests I don't mind sharing my woman with other men. Or how about the part where it states that I let you use my personal yacht for drug-fuelled parties? Or maybe the bit that says I came to your rescue yesterday because you could be carrying my child? And the soundbites in which your flatmate—Simone?—congratulates us on our impending nuptials were a genius touch. I must commend you on that. It ties everything up in a nice little bow, *non*?'

Shock careened through her as the oxygen left her lungs. Some of these paparazzi were in a class of their own, but even Ana couldn't believe they'd come up with such a preposterous story overnight.

She looked up, ready to defend herself, and saw his gaze fixed on the picture. 'I had no hand in any part of that story. But that's not what's bothering you, is it?'

'*Excusez moi?*'

'The picture bothers you way more than the article.'

Bastien's gaze iced over. 'You're in danger of stepping way over the line.'

'Why? Because this picture shows you looking at me as if you care? As if I get to you where no one else can?'

To the untrained eye he looked as most people saw him—a cool, suave businessman who was in complete control of his world. Sure, the tight jaw and the broad shoulders held an edge of danger that anyone would be a fool to ignore. But the concern, the touch of gentleness in his eyes, that same look she'd seen a long time ago when she was eight, was clear for her to see.

'You have a very active imagination, *cherie*,' he breathed.

'And *you* are not the icy, emotionless man you want the world to think you are. What are you so afraid of, Bastien?'

He didn't answer, merely speared her with his silver gaze as if trying to decipher whether she'd lost her mind. Hell, she might well have. She was tugging the tail of a dangerous beast.

'Bastien...'

'Let me be clear. Whatever you think you see in this photo does not exist. If you're scheming, making little plans in that beautiful head of yours, kill them dead—understand?'

Self-preservation kicked in, along with a healthy dose of anger.

Courage, Ana. 'I won't allow you to bully me, Bastien.'

He merely shrugged and strode for the door. 'Rest assured, any punishment I exact will be willingly accepted.'

'Dream on!'

He merely smiled. 'We'll see.'

She forced herself to take her time. She straightened her jacket, picked up the paper from the floor and placed it on the coffee table. Going to her bedroom, she scooped up her purse and the coat Mathilde had lent her. Shrugging it on, she fastened the belt and returned to the living room.

Bastien hadn't moved an inch. She slid past him and tried to ignore him as they rode the lift down.

The grand hotel's opulent foyer barely sparked her interest. It took every ounce of her willpower just to put one foot in front of the other, to follow Bastien's lengthy stride through the revolving doors to the car waiting at the kerb.

As they travelled along the cold streets of Geneva she struggled to come up with something to say, but appealing to Bastien's better nature would be a waste of time.

A quick glance showed he'd become engrossed in a stack of papers, his pen flying as he drew harsh lines through the document.

'Will you need me to speak to the board?'

The newspaper article had worsened her position. Firing her had become a real option now.

Bastien's lips firmed. 'The damage is already done.'

'What does that mean?'

'It means that now you get to reap the results of your little experiment.'

Her trepidation mounted as they drew up outside a large, elegant stone building. They'd left the gleaming, modern glass edifices behind a short while ago and entered the Old Town.

A liveried doorman complete with white gloves glided to the door and held it open. As she stepped into Bastien's lair Ana was aware that she could be leaving here with the course of her life very much altered.

Plush cream carpeting muffled their footsteps. Impressive paintings graced the walls—discreet, yet sure to make an impact on the super-rich clients lucky enough to be invited to invest with the Heidecker Corporation.

From behind a semi-circular reception desk a superbly coiffed receptionist greeted Bastien. 'The board members are assembled in the usual room, Monsieur Heidecker.'

He nodded. '*Merci*, Chloe. Can you tell Tatiana to meet us outside the boardroom?'

'Of course.' Her glance at Ana held unabashed curiosity as she picked up the phone to do Bastien's bidding.

He stepped into the lift and pressed a button. 'Tatiana's my PA. She'll make you comfortable while I'm in the meeting.'

Irritation surged through her. 'So I'm expected to just cool my heels? I could've stayed at the hotel.'

'We've already had this conversation. Where I go, you go,' he reiterated arrogantly.

'You're really enjoying this, aren't you?' she snapped.

'Why the sudden eagerness to present yourself to the board? I seem to recall you jumping out of a moving car to avoid coming here.' His eyes skimmed over her. 'You've even gone to great lengths to improve your appearance. Why is that, Miss Duval?'

'Do you always jump to the worst possible conclusions about everyone, or am I just flavour of the month?'

His brows merely lifted a fraction.

'Of course it wouldn't have occurred to you that I want this over and done with so I can get on with my life?'

A cynical smile twisted his sensual lips. 'Missing the thrill of the limelight?'

'No—just eager to get away from you and your warped ideas about me. I can't help but feel the more time I spend in your presence, the more I risk contamination from your twisted impressions of the human race.'

If she'd thought his gaze back in her hotel room could freeze water, his expression now sent a jagged bolt of apprehension through her. He lunged for her, strong hands hauling her up until only her toes touched the floor of the lift.

'A word of advice, *cherie*. Learn to pick your battles wisely.'

Afterwards Ana reckoned she must have gone slightly insane. Just for a few seconds. Because even she couldn't understand her compulsive need to goad him further.

'Or what, Bastien? You'll punish me for getting under your skin again?' The words slipped out before she could stop them.

With lightning speed he had her caged against the back wall of the lift. His mouth crushed hers, his tongue forcing its way into her mouth before she could draw half a breath. Molten heat scalded her from head to toe, sending a rush of sensation so heady she groaned with the sheer pleasure of it.

The sound seemed to galvanise Bastien. His hands bracketed her, his powerful body imprisoning her. From chest to knee, every muscle of his hard, streamlined physique was imprinted against hers as he devoured her lips.

When his tongue slid boldly against hers liquid fire shot through her bloodstream to pool low in her pelvis. The sensation was alien, but so exquisitely delightful that Ana whimpered. Again, the sound triggered something in Bastien.

He surged closer, rolled his hips until the unmistakable force of his arousal lay hot and heavy against her belly. A wave of longing stole over her, sparking a yearning to reach for him, to touch him in a way that would appease the stark hunger.

His strong jaw abraded her palm. Glorying in the new and

exciting textures, she traced her fingers to his nape, slid her fingers through his hair once more. She didn't know she'd applied pressure until the kiss deepened, their tongues tangling in a frenzied dance that culminated in desperate gasps for air.

Bastien stared down at her, shock darkening his eyes. '*Mon Dieu*, how the hell do you do this to me?' he demanded thickly under his breath.

The guttural sound of his voice shivered along her nerves, tightening the pressure in her womb and turning her nipples into hard, painful buds of need. Need that demanded satisfaction. *Now.*

This time she rose to her toes of her own accord, her need to experience the power of his kiss paramount. Bastien reached for her—

'*Excusez moi, monsieur?*'

The voice was cheeky, almost amused.

Bastien's harsh exhalation fanned her heated cheek. He stepped back, but didn't release her. Over one broad shoulder Ana saw a statuesque redhead in the open doorway of the lift, peering at them over boxy designer glasses.

'Tatiana, give me a minute,' he rasped.

'*Mais oui*, Bastien. But I suggest that you don't keep the board waiting any longer.'

Her heavily accented response held even more amusement. With a twirl that wouldn't have been misplaced on a catwalk, she disappeared down the hall, leaving behind a cloud of expensive perfume.

He dropped his hands. The loss of his touch sent a cold shiver through Ana, but not quite enough to restore clarity. Mind fuzzy, she remained where she was, shaky, eternally grateful for the support of the wall.

And totally convinced she'd lost her mind.

How could she have kissed him like that? Have lost herself so spectacularly? And so publicly! Shame drenched her, finally erasing the last dregs of her rioting emotions.

But a niggling voice remained.

What if they hadn't been interrupted? Would she have lifted her leg and curved it over his hip the way he'd urged her to do on his boat? Would she have encouraged him to cup her aching breasts because Bastien touching them ranked among the most beautiful feelings in the whole world?

Dear God, no!

'You promised me this would never happen again.' Her voice held all the husky undercurrents of the emotions shimmering beneath her skin and none of the accusation she'd intended to heap on his head.

His eyes mocked her. 'No, I never made such a promise. And you decided not to wait for that gold-embossed invitation after all. You issued one of your own. I merely accepted,' he rasped.

'I did no such thing. You're truly despic—'

'Much as I'd like to stand here trading insults with you all day, I have a meeting to attend.' Grasping her elbow, he stepped out of the lift, took a short hallway until they reached a set of double doors. 'Through there is my office. Tatiana will make you comfortable and let you know if you're needed.'

Without a backward glance, he walked away.

Ana didn't know whether to be relieved or angry. Taking a deep breath, she opted for relief. Anger led to a loss of control. Loss of control led to hot, torrid exchanges of intense kisses that left her weak and needy.

Yes, relief was a much better emotion to hang on to.

She entered the office, where Tatiana sat behind an exquisite antique desk. Calling on her much-practised poise, Ana approached.

'I don't think we were introduced properly. I'm Ana Duval.'

'Tatiana—Bastien's slave,' the other woman joked. She indicated another set of doors. 'There's a sitting room through there. I'll bring coffee in a moment. But perhaps you'd prefer to use the facilities to…to freshen up a little?'

Ana followed Tatiana's gaze. Her coat had come undone,

along with several buttons of her top, and she could feel her carefully pinned-up hair sliding loosely against her nape.

With as much dignity as she could muster she smiled. 'Thank you.'

In the privacy of the bathroom she let out a shaky breath and gazed with horror at her dishevelled state. The cream silk top she'd tucked into her skirt had come untucked, its material crumpled where Bastien's body had crushed hers. Luckily her suit had sustained less damage. Fingers trembling, Ana tried to repair her attire as best she could.

Renewed shame seared her. Her lips were red and swollen, her lip-gloss long gone. Her cheeks were flushed and her eyes reflected an untamed look that made her gaze slither away in disgust.

Once again she'd let herself down. And this time she couldn't pretend that she hadn't wanted it to happen. Her fingers tingled from where she'd willingly grasped Bastien's nape and invited a deeper kiss.

It could never happen again.

She splashed cold water over her hands. She'd survived childhood with a mother who'd been bent on cruelty and humiliation at every stage. She'd grown up without the fundamental learning tools every child was entitled to and had still made a success of her life.

Surely she could overcome the raw temptation that was Bastien Heidecker?

It would never happen again.

Satisfied with that affirmation, she tugged her jacket back into place and returned to the sitting room with her head held high.

Bastien answered another inconsequential question, his frustration mounting as the subject of the DBH campaign was once again avoided by his chairman, Claude Delon. He curbed his need to glance to the left side of the room, where Ana had taken a seat five minutes ago. His fellow board members weren't as circumspect in hiding their interest.

He couldn't blame Delon for his volcanic mood. No, it was what had happened in the lift that roiled in his blood. His jaw tightened. He'd lost control. Again. He'd allowed her to goad him until the only sensible response had been to shut her up in the most ruthless way possible.

But even as the glaring error of that course of action taunted him he admitted how good shutting her up had felt. Her lips, soft but firm, had fought against his attempts to dominate, her tongue duelling with his in a curious mixture of defiance and innocence before yielding, kissing him back in a most pleasurable way.

How her soft moans had echoed like thunder through his veins… And the supple imprint of her body, the bones of her hips cradling his pelvis as if made to fit…

He slammed his open palm on the table, cheap satisfaction coursing through him when seven pairs of eyes jerked from Ana to him.

'We voted on the acquisition of the copper mine two days ago, so why are we discussing it again? In fact everything on the agenda has been covered except one item. Some of you might have nothing better than a round of golf planned after this meeting, but I have work to do.'

'You sound a little…stressed, Bastien. Perhaps the events of the last few days have taken their toll?' Delon suggested.

'The state of my health isn't up for discussion. Are you ready to vote?'

The older man spread his hands wide. 'We discussed this while we were waiting for you to arrive. After reading this morning's papers, we don't see the need to discuss this any further.'

He sensed Ana tense but refused to look her way. Since she'd walked in, chin high, her stride confident and sexy, she'd commanded too much attention. Witnessing the keen interest in more than one board member's expression, he'd felt something dark, dangerous and agonisingly twisted course through his veins.

Her clothes, although respectable—demure, even, compared to her previous attire—didn't mask Ana's raw sexuality.

Bastien's fist clenched against the throbbing in his groin and he curbed the impulse to snarl at the wily old chairman. One error of judgement was enough for one day.

'What's that supposed to mean?'

'It means that ultimately the story and the photo, while we wouldn't normally like to draw that sort of attention to the company, was a stroke of genius. I assume that you've seen the surge in share price this morning?'

Bastien's mood blackened even more. 'Of course I have—but I find it preposterous that you would attribute the surge to a picture in the tabloids.'

'You underestimate the power of the media,' Claude replied, his eyes flicking to Ana. 'Perhaps as much as you underestimate the power of a *liaison romantique*.'

Ana made a strange little sound—a cross between a snort and a cough. He finally looked her way, slicing her a look that straightened the amused curve of her mouth. When she lifted a brow in silent challenge he ground his teeth, cursing the memory of her seductive warmth pressed against him, the subtle thrust of her tongue against his, which was pulling him from reality.

What was wrong with him?

He knew how lethal she was to his control and yet he couldn't stop his body from reacting like a randy sailor on shore leave.

Turning his head, he concentrated on the old man. 'You must be going blind, Claude. There is no such—'

Ana spoke up. 'Bastien, I think what your chairman is trying to say is don't look a gift horse in the mouth.'

A smattering of amusement rolled around the conference room.

'If the picture is helping the DBH range to thrive, despite

the hit it took yesterday, surely that can't be a bad thing?' she went on.

'*Précisément*. Women across the globe are reading the newspaper this morning, sighing over the picture and wishing they were in Mademoiselle Duval's shoes. That's already translating to a surge in profits. If you ask me, your little courthouse adventure was quite ingenious. Perhaps we should make Ana an honorary member of the board.'

Bastien's gaze slid back to her and he saw a wide smile spread across her face. Every male breath in the room had caught at the incredible sight.

His teeth ground harder. 'Perhaps you're forgetting the small matter of your trial?'

Her smile dimmed and her throat moved in a delicate swallow. Her eyes blazed as they locked on his, a determined fire lighting their depths. 'I'm quite confident I'll be proved innocent by the time the trial rolls around.'

'Don't make promises you may not be able to keep, Miss Duval.'

'I'm seriously committed to finding out the truth behind what happened and to making your campaign a success. If I fail you can do with me what you will,' she replied, a tinge of anger in her voice.

His gaze dropped to the soft pout of her mouth and another rush of heat speared through him. For a single moment he hated himself for wanting her to fail just so he could bend her to his will, take what she'd unwittingly offered.

But then the thought of Ana behind bars, locked away from the world, slid through his mind. Something tightened in his chest, growing stronger as a memory long buried surfaced out of nowhere. It pierced so deep his breath faltered.

Ana—eight years old, running down the steps at Verbier to show him something. She'd always been doing that…plucking random things from the house or the garden to show him, unwilling to accept that he just wanted to be left alone.

Alone to deal with his father's betrayal; with his mother's

abandonment. Alone to grieve the loss of the perfect family unit he'd taken for granted.

Slowly Bastien glanced around the room. He'd forgotten he had an audience. The same way he'd forgotten where he was when he'd kissed her earlier.

Jaw tightening, he rose. 'This meeting is over,' he said into the curious silence.

Chairs screeched on wooden floors one by one and the room emptied.

Then he took a deep sustaining breath and turned to her. 'What the hell did you think you were playing at?'

'What?'

'You were supposed to remain silent until you were called on to speak.'

One elegant brow rose. 'You mean like some sort of marionette, ready to perform on command?'

Heat rose up his neck. 'I didn't say that.'

'Then what exactly did you mean?'

He shoved a hand through his hair, words completely failing him. Striding to the drinks tray set in a corner of the conference room, he splashed vintage cognac into a crystal tumbler and sent the fiery liquid coursing down his throat.

It was only the afternoon…just…but he didn't care.

'Is that a celebratory drink or a *Damn, Ana isn't getting fired* drink?'

Bastien whirled. She stood behind him, her arms folded across her slender midriff, the picture of composure. Or was it quiet triumph?

For the first time he'd let his emotions get the better of him in the boardroom. He wanted to see her ruffled, shaken, off balance. The way *he* was feeling.

'It's a *Where the hell has my sanity gone?* drink. You want one?'

'No, thanks. I know where mine is.'

'Do you? Then *bravo*.' He raised his glass to her.

She frowned and drew closer, those long, shapely legs capturing his attention as she moved, bringing a seductive scent that instantly surrounded him. A few feet away she stopped, doe eyes wide and alluring.

'What's really going on, Bastien?'

'Why do you insist on using my name when I've made it clear it's off-limits?'

She flinched and the band around his chest tightened.

Hell...

'Because, despite those horrid vibes you give out, I still want to remain civil.' An intimate smile curved her perfect, pouting lips.

Lust rose to mingle with anger. Bastien wanted to reach for her, demonstrate his ire in unmistakably graphic terms. Instead he reached behind him, grabbed the bottle, poured another measure of cognac and raised the glass to his lips.

'I don't need your civility, Miss Duval. But if you carry on like this I may well take you up on the invitation you keep issuing. Maybe that will get you from underneath my skin once and for all.'

CHAPTER FIVE

SEVERAL IMAGES FLASHED across her brain, each one more graphic than the last. Furiously, she tried to blink them away, praying that the fire spiralling upwards from her belly wouldn't engulf her whole body.

He took his time swirling his drink, savouring a taste of the amber liquid, before he quirked one amused eyebrow at her. 'Nothing to say?'

'It's not going to work.'

That stopped him. 'Excuse me?'

'No matter how much you try to rile me, it's not going to work.'

'*Mon Dieu*, you're as stubborn as you were when you were eight years old.'

She nodded. 'And you've become an expert at hiding your feelings—albeit under a veneer of brusqueness that grates, but I see right through you.'

He slammed the glass down, stalked to where she stood and glared down at her. 'What exactly do you think you see?'

Ana fought the urge to caress that tight jaw. 'After all this time you're still hurting. And don't bother denying it. You don't speak to your father unless you absolutely have to. I heard one of your board members ask you how he was doing when I came into the room. You shut him down. You blame your father for what happened too, don't you?'

'Of *course* I blame him!' he shouted. 'Do you think I should just forgive him for what he did?'

'I think you need to find a way to put it behind you so it doesn't consume you like this.'

He laughed, the sound like chips of ice being crunched underfoot. 'How very Zen of you. Have you done the same with your mother?'

Ana sucked in a painful breath. 'I've tried. She refuses to admit she did anything wrong.'

'And yet you still entertain her in your life—even employ her as your manager? Would I be wrong in thinking that on some level you're okay with what she did?'

She flinched. 'Yes, you would be!'

'Then what are you doing about it?' he challenged.

About to speak, she froze, unprepared for the slap of realisation that she'd lived with her mother's behaviour for so long she did silently accept it. 'I don't claim to have all the answers, but I know cutting your father off isn't one of them.'

'You're right—you don't have the answers. So don't throw stones. And do *not* speak to me about what happened sixteen years ago. As of now, that subject is closed.' His voice was taut with suppressed anger.

Whirling away, he strode to the window. His tense shoulders bunched as he slid both hands into his trouser pockets. Dappled sunlight framed his head in a golden halo. Ana stared, astounded by her inability to stop looking at him. But this time she saw past it to the hurt boy beneath. And her heart broke for him.

'How can it be when it colours everything you do?'

A breath shuddered out of him. '*Mon Dieu*, Ana, I'm trying. Just let it go. Please.'

She swallowed hard and blinked back threatening tears. 'Okay, I'll let it go. For now.'

After several minutes he turned. 'Your little stunt with the newspaper has paid off. I suggest you focus on what happens next.'

'What does that mean?'

'It means I'm relocating the ad campaign here,' he said.

'What?' Surprise jerked through her. 'Why? The venue in Scotland has been arranged and it's all set to go.'

'Since my presence is required where *you* are, I'd rather stay in a place where I can be guaranteed there won't be a repeat of any suggestive newspaper articles. There's very little press intrusion in Switzerland.'

'So for the next three weeks I'm your prisoner?'

His eyebrows rose. 'You'd rather return to London and feed more stories to the papers?'

'I want to go home.'

Despite reassuring herself that she could control her feelings around him, her every instinct protested against spending any more time in Bastien's disturbing company. The last shoot had overrun a whole week. If the pattern repeated itself she could be here for a long time, perhaps even until her trial. Here with this man who couldn't fail to elicit intense, dangerous emotions from her.

'That's not going to happen.'

Anger exploded inside her. 'You can't do this!'

Her outburst brought a frown. 'I'm willing to concede that the article may have helped save my company, Miss Duval, but I won't be giving the press any more fodder for their gossip rags.'

'Seriously—would you stop with the *Miss Duval* nonsense? It sounds ridiculous, considering we've…' Ana faltered. Had she seriously been about to invite him to call her by her first name because they'd had their hands all over each other not once but twice in the last twenty-four hours?

She'd truly lost her mind.

'Considering we've what? Been intimate?'

'What happened between us wasn't *intimacy*,' she denied through stiff lips.

A grim parody of a smile curved his lips. 'I agree. It was undeniably primal, and irritating as hell, but it was not intimacy.'

Somewhere deep inside her something cracked. Something she hadn't even known existed. 'No, it wasn't.'

He gave her a quizzical glance before striding to his desk. He reached for a leather-bound file. 'I'm glad we're agreed. Tatiana will get the driver to take you back to the hotel. Be ready to leave at six.'

'Leave? Where are we going?' she asked.

'My château. That's where the shoot is now taking place. We'll stay there until it's wrapped. Oh, and Ana?'

'Yes?'

'I'm trusting you not to do anything foolish like attempt to leave.'

'I'm so honoured by your trust,' she returned sarcastically.

His sensual mouth compressed and he sat down, reached for his phone and swung his chair towards the window.

Ana felt as though she'd been released from the heady power of a vortex. Yet the relief she craved was absurdly missing. Surely she couldn't *want* to lock horns with Bastien?

Irritated with herself, she retrieved her bag and left his office, ignoring the hypnotic husk of his voice as he conversed in flawless French.

'Are you ready to leave?' Tatiana's smile oozed enviable confidence.

Forcing herself to focus, Ana nodded. 'Yes, thank you.'

Back in her hotel suite, Ana threw down her handbag and pulled the pins from her hair. It seemed a lifetime ago when she'd left here, fearing the worst. The axe hadn't fallen as she'd expected, yet her instincts warned that she faced a darker threat.

She hated the idea that she had to remain in Switzerland, but she silently conceded that Bastien was right. What good would returning home do aside from setting the paparazzi on her tail again?

Going to the window, she opened the curtain and drank in the view. A towering jet of water shot into the sky from the jetty across the lake, its cascading drops creating breathtaking prisms of light.

Craving a modicum of freedom, she dashed to the bedroom

and changed into the clothes she'd worn on the plane. Defiantly, she wore a bra underneath the top this time. The coat covered the worst of the daring slashes and minimised her exposure.

She left the hotel, making sure to keep it in sight at all times. Using the jet of water as her landmark, she walked along the bank, hoping the fresh air would clear her thoughts.

Unbidden, Bastien's face rose into her mind: the haunted look in his eyes when she mentioned what happened sixteen years ago. That he carried baggage from that time was fairly obvious. So did she, after all. But Bastien was lucky. His parents had stayed together. She hadn't been so lucky. Her mother's erratic behaviour and bitter rants had worsened after their winter in Verbier because Bastien's father had returned to his wife.

His family had survived Lily Duval's toxic intrusion. He should be celebrating. She and her father hadn't been so lucky.

Her phone trilled. She seized on it in relief—until she saw the number.

Ana contemplated letting it go to voicemail. But her mother would only call back. Lily didn't like to be ignored.

'Lily.' Ana had been forbidden from calling her Mother the day she'd turned nine.

'I see you've landed herself in a bit of a pickle,' her mother drawled in carefully cultivated upper-class tones.

'I'm fine. Thank you for asking.'

Ana had trained herself long ago not to listen for any softening in her mother's voice but she found herself doing so now, her conversations with Bastien having rubbed at the barrier she'd placed around her heart where her mother was concerned.

'You're a Duval. Life will knock you down but you have to learn to bounce back,' Lily snapped.

Her heart clenched painfully. Again she thought back to her conversation in Bastien's office and her grip tightened on the phone. Was she being a hypocrite by letting her mother get away with treating her so badly?

'So your less than loving treatment of me all these years was supposed to teach me a *lesson*?'

Taut silence greeted her daring question, followed by a haughty, 'I have no idea what you're talking about, dear.'

Another jagged arrow of pain lanced through her. 'Did you ever stop to think I might need a shoulder to cry on before I took my next lesson?'

Her mother laughed. 'Even if I wanted to offer a shoulder you'd never take it.'

Ana froze. 'How would you know, since you've never offered it?'

Again a small pause, before Lily sighed. 'I may be blind to some things but not to everything, dear. But, be that as it may, I called to offer my advice. If you're thinking of starting anything with Bastien Heidecker I suggest you think twice.'

It took a few seconds to arrange her reeling thoughts. 'Thank you, but the advice isn't necessary.'

'That picture in the paper suggests otherwise.'

Ana exhaled sharply at the reminder that her momentary loss of composure was now streaming across the world. 'I'm not thinking of starting anything with anyone.'

'That's good. Take it from one who knows: the Heidecker men are ruthless liars. They'll string you along until they get what they want from you, then leave you high and dry.' Unmistakeble bitterness coated her words.

'So you take no responsibility for what happened sixteen years ago?'

Ana had expected a swift denial, and was shocked when her mother made a quickly veiled sound of distress. 'Believe it or not, I do.'

Ana halted in surprise. 'You *do*?'

'Hindsight is a wonderful thing—so, yes, I wish things had turned out differently. Anyway, the thing to do is look forward.'

Ana closed her eyes. 'Well, I can't just yet. The past is ruining my life.' She tried for a light-hearted tone despite the vice squeezing her heart.

'Then don't do as I did. Take the lesson you need from it but don't hang on to it.'

This unexpected morsel of advice made Ana's breath catch. 'Are you okay?'

'Of course I am. Or I will be as soon as I find another gig. I've left the show,' she added, her attempt at flippancy not quite hitting the mark.

'Why? What happened?'

'The director was a bore. His artistic vision was totally wrong.'

'The truth, Lily. What really happened?'

Her mother sucked in a shaky breath. 'He told me he loved me... Of course it turned out to be lies. All lies.'

Against her will, a lump formed in Ana's throat. 'I see.'

'You *see*? That's all you have to say?'

'I can't pretend to be surprised.'

Her mother gave a shocked gasp. 'I don't know what I was thinking...calling you for support—'

'Lily, listen to me. You're worth so much more than what you let happen to you. Why don't you take your own advice—?'

'It's that man, isn't it? Turning you against me!'

'Bastien has nothing to do with this.' But his voice echoed at the back of her mind all the same...

'Well, don't call me when Bastien kicks you to the kerb. Just remember I warned you—all men are bastards.' The line went dead.

Not all men... Some men could be gentle when they chose... could make you feel safe...

A cool mist touched her face. With a start, she realised she'd reached the water jet.

Turning around, she headed back to the hotel, the joy of her walk gone. *Had* she silently condoned her mother's behaviour all this time? Enabled her, even, by continuing to support her just to keep the lines of communication open...the secret hope of a connection?

Her phone rang again. She stared at the number and breathed a sigh of relief.

'Papá!' She summoned a smile, her world brightening a little.

'I heard something on the news about you. I'm worried,' he said after they'd exchanged pleasantries.

She bit her lip and quickly summarised what had happened to her, knowing that her father didn't keep up with current affairs on his dig in Colombia but not wanting to risk him finding out anyway.

'How did this happen, Ana?' he asked in the softly modulated voice that could turn steely when needed.

'I don't know, but I didn't do it.'

'*Sí*, I know that,' he said impatiently. 'But you need to find out who wishes you such harm and deal with it.'

His unequivocal belief in her innocence brought a lump to her throat. Taking a few seconds, she cleared it. 'I intend to. Um…about the internship…'

'Make things right in your world. I will make things right here.'

The lump threatened to choke her again. 'Thank you, Papá.'

She returned to her room, still caught in a cross-current of emotion but forcing herself to shrug it off and deal with her predicament. She might be stuck in Switzerland for the time being, but she wasn't helpless.

Two hours later she threw her phone down in frustration and hugged her knees. The few trusted friends she'd made in the business couldn't shed any light on what had happened.

Her stomach rumbled, reminding her that she'd gone all day without a meal. She reached for the phone again just as a knock sounded on her door.

Glancing down at herself, she debated whether to change. The thought of donning her suit again made her grimace. Bastien had already seen her like this. And she was wearing a bra this time.

With a deep breath that failed to replenish her oxygen-deprived lungs, she pulled the door open.

He stood tall and imposing, his face impassive as he surveyed her. She'd expected another disparaging comment about her state of dress, but his gaze merely skimmed over her loose hair and unmade-up face.

'Have you eaten?' he asked.

'No.'

'Dinner is being delivered to my suite in ten minutes. Will you join me?'

'I was just about to order Room Service.' She didn't want to risk going head to head with him again; their last exchange was still very vivid in her mind.

A smile flashed on and off. 'I've saved you the trouble, then. We have things to discuss. I'll see you in five minutes.' Without waiting for a reply, he sauntered off.

Knowing it was pointless to argue, she returned to her bedroom, applied a coat of lip-gloss, slipped on high-heeled sandals and brushed her hair. Tucking her key card into her pocket, she left her suite.

His was the only other suite on this floor, and when she pushed the open door wider he motioned for her to enter.

Decorated in identical tones of gold and blue, his suite was much grander than hers. Gilt-edged mirrors adorned the walls and an impressive fireplace rested beneath an ornate mantelpiece. Gold velvet curtains had been caught back with blue velvet rope, and beyond the window the lights on the lake twinkled in the falling dusk. But what caught her eye, as it had earlier in the day, was the plume of water, now backlit with a stunning array of lights.

'What *is* that fountain?'

'The Jet d'Eau. The highest water fountain in the world.' He spoke in a clipped staccato, as if he had other things on his mind.

About to comment on the jet's beauty, Ana stopped and turned. The intensity of his stare made the hairs twitch on her nape.

'This was left downstairs for you.' He held a square brown envelope in his hand.

Ana's mind blanked for a second, then she remembered. 'Why do *you* have it?'

'The concierge said it was delivered moments before I came. I told him I'd deliver it to you.'

'How kind of you.' She held out her hand. 'Can I have it?'

'What's in the envelope, Ana?' he asked tersely.

Shock battled with a sensation curiously similar to a delicious thrill of pleasure. A second later she realised Bastien hadn't even noticed that he'd used her first name. Out of nowhere came a deep yearning to hear him call her Ana again. But not like that. She wanted him to say her name and mean it. She wanted him to say her name with pleasure.

Ruthlessly, she pushed the fanciful thought away. That was never going to happen. Desolation settled deep within her.

'You open it,' she prompted softly.

A flicker of surprise lit his eyes. Perhaps he'd been expecting her to fight him. But some time in the last few hours Ana had decided that if they were to spend the next three weeks together she couldn't keep locking horns with him. Her control wouldn't sustain the battering.

'If you want to know what's in the envelope, open it.'

He ripped it open immediately. Ana watched his eyes widen as he encountered the cold plastic. His gaze shot down and he stared at the object in his hand.

'I asked your company doctor this morning if he could replace my inhaler. He promised to have it delivered here this afternoon.'

The doorbell rang. Bastien didn't seem to hear it. He continued to stare at the inhaler.

Ana went to walk past him to get the door. His hand shot out and grabbed her arm. A frown creased his brow.

'Ana...'

She sighed. 'I'm sorry if that disappoints you. But it really is just an inhaler.'

The bell rang again. She pulled at her arm.

He let her go.

With a cold lump of despair lodged in her chest, Ana answered the door.

Bastien raked a hand through his hair, the unsettling feeling from this afternoon surging higher. He glanced down again at the inhaler. The stark reminder that Ana had a potentially life-threatening condition made his chest tighten.

All afternoon he'd tried not to think about their conversation—tried not to admit to himself that her words held any truth. No one had dared challenge him on why he refused to let emotion rule his life. Until her.

He'd remained in a foul mood right up until he'd been handed that package downstairs. Then it had taken a turn for the worse.

Remorse stung deep now, unnerving him further. When had he ever felt the need to apologise for anything? Yet now the urge to make things right needled him.

He stood aside to let the waiter wheel the trolley into the dining room. Ana followed, her lush figure swaying seductively. She was wearing those damned jeans again. The sight of the exposed lower curve of her bottom made him swallow. *Hard.* Fire roared through his blood as his gaze touched on more bare flesh.

His gaze travelled upwards, taking in the indentation of her slender waist and the golden triangles of skin exhibited there too. When he saw the straps of her flesh-coloured bra the fire raged into an inferno. Yesterday she'd forgone the bra—no doubt to avoid a fashion *faux pas* the way some women went without underwear to avoid a visible panty line. So why did the sight of the bra inflame his senses so much more than its absence had?

He forced his gaze away from temptation. Unfortunately the waiter had no such compunction, his gaze openly appreciative.

'*C'est tout,*' Bastien snarled. He stalked him to the door, barely resisting the urge to slam it, and returned to find Ana seated, lifting the lid on the dishes.

'This looks delicious. I'm absolutely starving.'

'Then help yourself,' he replied. His voice was terse but he couldn't help it. Shock, confusion and intense desire tended to do that to a man. Sustained for long periods of time, who knew its repercussions?

'Would you like me to serve you?'

For one hot, inappropriate moment Bastien's mind lit on a completely different interpretation of that question. The images that bombarded him made him suck in a strained breath. He looked down at the plate her hand, at the spoon poised over the rosti and grilled lamb.

Reeling his thoughts in under fierce guard, he sat down next to her and put her inhaler on the table.

'I owe you an apology.'

The spoon wavered in her hand. Reaching across, he gently removed it from her grasp.

'Let me.' He spooned several helpings onto her plate, set it down in front of her and served himself. 'I had no right to question you about the package. *Je suis désolé.*'

Her eyes widened and she nodded. 'Apology accepted.' She gave a short laugh. 'The last two days have been little…challenging—although I can't say I would've done the same in your shoes.'

Bastien grimaced. Knowing he deserved the barbed accusation, he picked up and held out the wine bottle. At her nod, he uncorked it and poured the rich burgundy into her glass. Filling his own glass, he drank deep.

She took a mouthful of food and groaned. 'This is seriously good!' Her gaze dropped to his plate. 'You haven't tasted yours yet.'

'No,' he replied, and drank more wine. *Mon Dieu*, he was turning into a raging alcoholic—and all because of the woman sitting across from him. The woman who challenged him, made him question himself and the presence of the ache deep inside he'd thought he'd smothered for good.

'Well, don't blame me if I eat all of it.'

'Go ahead. A woman who doesn't complain about piling on the pounds at the mere sight of food makes a refreshing change.'

Her husky self-conscious laugh played havoc with his equilibrium. 'I didn't actually mean that. I'm not that much of a pig.'

'Trust me, a pig is the last thing I think of when I look at you.'

Her eyes rounded.

Advising himself that it was best not to keep looking into those captivating brown depths, he resolutely picked up his fork. 'What's likely to trigger an attack?'

'My asthma?'

He nodded.

'I've only suffered one serious attack, so I'd say I'm generally risk-free.' She shrugged, causing one sleeve to slip off her shoulder. 'But sometimes in the spring, if the pollen count is high, it gets a bit uncomfortable. Heavy smoke isn't great for me either.'

Bastien frowned. 'So you don't *know* how susceptible you are?'

'I know what to stay away from and what situations I'll be okay in.'

'Yet that didn't stop you from putting yourself in danger by attending your friend's party?'

'I can't live my life in fear of an attack,' she said, after swallowing another mouthful.

Bastien abandoned his meal and picked up his glass. 'No, but—'

'I took my inhaler with me,' she interrupted, glaring at him.

He was being heavy-handed again. He looked into his glass, slowly swirling his drink, and forced himself to calm down. 'And we all know how *that* turned out.'

When she didn't reply immediately, he looked up. Her lips were pursed into a firm line and she'd paled a little. One hand absently toyed with the stem of her glass as she stonily examined the contents of her plate.

'We're having a nice meal, Bastien. Don't ruin it.'

Bastien cursed under his breath and set his glass down. 'Have you packed yet?'

Her gaze returned warily to his. 'I didn't *un*pack because I didn't think I'd be staying beyond today.'

'Then we can leave directly after dinner.'

She nodded. 'Fine by me. Where's your château?'

'It's in Vaud—on the shores of Lac Léman.'

'Will anyone else be there?'

'My estate staff live on the grounds, but otherwise we'll be alone. Does that concern you?' Part of him wished that it would—that the notion would unsettle her the way he'd felt unsettled all day long.

She returned his gaze, her eyes wide. 'No. Why would it?'

'Because you're biting your lip again. That tells me something's bothering you. Are you worried that the moment we're alone we'll be tempted to do dirty little things to each other?'

'Of course not. We're perfectly capable of restraining ourselves.'

His smile felt tight. 'If you say so.'

CHAPTER SIX

ANA PRETENDED INTEREST in the scenery until darkness limited her view to the tall trees lining the road leading to Bastien's château.

Château D'Or, he'd called it. The golden castle.

The place where they might be tempted to 'do dirty little things to each other…'

Her fingers dug into her seat in a futile attempt to stop wondering what those dirty little things would entail, but her pulse continued to race, and that insistent throbbing between her legs was growing by the minute.

Shaking herself out of the weakening sensation, she turned to him, carefully averting her gaze from his confident hands gripping the steering wheel.

'How much longer?' she asked, thankful when her voice came out steady.

'Another ten minutes should see us there. Tired?'

His genuine concern made her relax slightly.

'It's been a long day.'

She dragged a hand through her hair, lifted its heavy weight off her neck. Twirling it into a thick rope, she coiled it around her fingers. When he followed the movement she paused, but his gaze returned to the road in the next instant.

Releasing her breath, she continued playing with the strands. 'I called around to find out if anyone knew more about what happened at the nightclub.'

Silver eyes briefly speared hers. 'And?'

'No one knows anything.'

His brows lifted. 'Does that surprise you?'

'Frankly, yes. Normally gossip like that spreads like wildfire.'

He didn't reply for several minutes, his gaze glued to the dark, winding road. Finally, he nodded. 'I have a firm of investigators I use for due diligence. I'll have them look into it.'

The unexpected offer made her breath catch. 'Really? Thank you, Bastien.' On pure impulse she reached for his arm. 'I really appreciate it.'

Packed muscle flexed beneath her touch, his cotton shirt and dark sweater no barrier against the warmth that seeped through to her fingers. Instant fiery desire made her fingers curl, and the irrational urge to keep touching him unfurled inside her like a driving, persistent hunger.

She didn't know how long she stayed like that. Seconds. Minutes. Time lost meaning and rational thought fled as she stared at his profile—his gorgeous face, his taut cheekbones, those unspeakably long, golden lashes and the lush mouth that had taken such powerful control of hers. His strong throat...

And his tense jaw...within which a muscle flicked.

Dirty little things...dirty little things...

Ana snatched back her hand, certain she was sliding into madness. 'I'm sorry. I shouldn't have... I didn't mean to—'

'Don't apologise, *cherie*. Believe it or not, I don't hate it when you touch me. If anything, I like it a little too much.'

His husky rasp cut through her words. She gasped, but before she could reply he continued.

'We're here.'

They drove through tall iron gates housed in a stone arch that looked as if it had been around since medieval times. Endless trees stretched over them like silent sentinels as they made their way up the drive.

Unbidden, a shiver passed through her. The feeling of foreboding she'd experienced this morning returned—forcefully this time. Calling herself all kinds of fool for entertaining it, she brushed it away.

Once the photo shoot and her trial were over she'd be free of Bastien, free to fulfil her dreams. Perhaps this sense of standing on the edge of a precipice was merely subconscious exhilaration at her impending freedom.

Clinging to that, Ana straightened in her seat.

At her first glimpse, she knew why the château had gained its name.

It stood like a shimmering mirage on top of a small hill, a wonderful surprise at the end of a copse of trees. Bathed in mellow light, the yellow stone would look golden in any light—day or night.

'Wow, it's breathtaking.'

'Yes, it is.' He turned off the ignition. 'Welcome to Château D'Or,' he said, and thrust his door open.

She followed suit, unable to take her eyes off the stunning building. Set on three storeys, with elegant dormer windows that would give amazing views over the valley they'd just climbed out of, the château looked like every girl's childhood dream castle. It came complete with a west-facing flagged and turreted tower built to capture the perfect sunset.

A large wooden door hewn from oak opened, drawing Ana's attention from the tower. A small-framed woman greeted them, her smile warming when she saw Bastien.

'This is Chantal. She manages the château and its gardens with her husband. Their son and daughter-in-law help in the stables and look after the horses.'

'You have horses?' Ana asked, after returning Chantal's greeting.

Bastien paused where he was unloading their luggage. 'You ride?' Surprise tinged his voice.

'I used to. We lived on a ranch in Brazil for six months.'

He tensed. 'We?'

She ignored the tautness in his voice. 'Lily and I spent time there.' Until her mother's Brazilian lover ditched her.

But by then Ana had had a love of horses firmly entrenched in her heart.

'Why did you leave?' Bastien asked. The strain was gone from his voice, had been replaced by gentle speculation.

'It didn't work out. What kind of horses do you keep?' she asked quickly, eager to escape the subject of her mother.

He slammed the boot shut, picked up their cases. 'The best kind.' He smiled. 'If you're really interested, I'll show you in the morning.'

Again his unexpected offer threw her. 'Yes, please.'

The next half-hour was spent touring the château, and each high-ceilinged, history-rich room revealed was even more spectacular than the last. By the time Chantal showed Ana to her room—complete with lace-curtained four-poster bed—she'd fallen in love with Château D'Or.

Bastien entered with her suitcase just as the housekeeper left. 'Is everything satisfactory?'

'More than—thanks.'

'If you're hungry Chantal can fix you a light meal?' he offered.

'No, I'm fine. Thanks.'

He stood there, hands in his back pockets. He'd changed after dinner into a pair of jeans and boots and over his shirt he wore a grey cashmere sweater. With his windblown hair he easily carried off a rugged look that might have graced the cover of any fashion magazine.

She looked up and her gaze collided with his. His lips quirked in a parody of a smile. She'd been caught staring again. Would she never learn?

'I think I'll have an early night.'

He nodded and turned for the door. 'Good idea. Anything that keeps you out of trouble is most welcome,' he drawled.

Unable to resist, she grabbed the nearest pillow and flung it at his back, then giggled madly when he turned, surprise darkening his grey eyes.

He picked up the pillow and walked back to her. 'The trouble with pillow fights, *cherie*, is that they lead to so much else. So pick your battles carefully.' He pressed the pillow into her chest and drew her arms around it. '*Bon nuit*, Ana,' he murmured, then left.

Ana sank onto the bed, her breath fizzing out of her like a deflating balloon. Her body thrummed with a thousand volts of electricity, and her whirling mind was in no state to settle down to sleep.

He might have left her room, but she could still feel him—could still smell Bastien. His presence dominated her thoughts, charged the very air she breathed.

For a few hours Bastien had been civil, even gentle at times. His apology at dinner and his offer to investigate her drug charge had made her wonder what he might be like if they didn't have such a chequered and miserable past.

But then the foreboding returned—thick and more urgent than before. Perhaps they were better off as they were, because she has an unshakable feeling that he would be much more dangerous to her emotional wellbeing unless she kept him at arm's length.

The sound of a car door slamming woke her. Stretching, Ana opened her eyes, disorientated until memory rushed back.

Thrusting aside the sheets, she went to the window.

Lake Geneva gleamed like a silver ribbon, so close she could almost reach out and touch it. Its rich green banks meandered until they disappeared from view. On the other side stunning vistas gave way to a low mountain range behind which she spotted the familiar summit of Mont Blanc in France.

The sight of the departing car drew her attention back to the grounds.

An overnight guest? Realising she had no idea whether Bastien had a girlfriend or not, she stared after the car, the idea sending an inexplicable lance of pain through her.

A knock on her door made her jump.

Ana glanced down at herself. Her negligee was way too

risqué for public consumption. Diving into the bathroom, she grabbed a robe, shrugged it on and answered the door.

Bastien held a large suitcase in his hand. He strode in and dropped it at the foot of the bed. 'In here you'll find a more favourable selection of clothes,' he announced. 'Make use of them and meet me downstairs in ten minutes.'

'Excuse me?'

He faced her, his cool gaze conducting a leisurely survey of her before meeting her eyes. 'Which bit needs further explanation?'

'Er…all of it. Including the part where you say good morning, like most civilised people do.'

He leaned his shoulder against one bedpost, his gaze going to the rumpled bed before turning to hers. '*Bonjour*, Ana. Did you sleep well?'

Her heart lurched. He'd used her name again. With no hint of mockery. Okay, maybe a tiny hint of mockery.

'Yes, I did—thanks for asking.' She strove for a casual reply. 'Did you?'

He raised an eyebrow. '*Oui, merci.* Does that conclude our small talk?'

She nodded at the suitcase. 'Maybe. Care to explain why you've brought me clothes?'

He straightened and headed for the door. 'I would've thought there was no explanation needed. Get dressed and meet me downstairs.'

'No.'

He gave a pained sigh and turned. 'Are you always this trying first thing in the morning?'

Clutching the lapels of her robe together, she shrugged. 'I wouldn't be if you gave me a straight answer.'

'You expressed an interest in my horses. Unless you expect to go riding wearing skimpy clothes, and risk catching your death of pneumonia, your only option is to wear more sensible attire.'

Something treacherous melted inside her. 'So you went shopping this morning?'

He smiled and Ana's heart galloped wildly.

'Like most men, the thought of spending hours choosing clothes makes me want to stick pins in my eyes. No, you have Tatiana to thank for your little windfall.'

'Oh…thanks, but I can't accept them.'

His smile disappeared. Slowly he retraced his steps until he stood in front of her. 'You wouldn't be leaping to the same conclusions you did on the plane, would you?' he asked softly.

Her face flamed. 'No, of course not. But I'm not in the habit of accepting charity—'

'What about gifts from friends?' he demanded, and then he frowned, his nostrils flaring with a touch of discomfort.

She forced herself not to gape. '*Are* we friends, Bastien?'

'I'm attempting to be less…ogre-like.'

She laughed. 'That frown you're wearing makes a mockery of the attempt.'

His lips pursed. 'Fine. If you feel so strongly about my gift you can return the clothes when you leave.'

Ana bit her lip, trying and failing not to read too much into this change overcoming Bastien. He had gentleness in him. She knew that. But history had taught her that it was foolhardy to lower her guard.

Without warning he pressed his thumb over her mouth, stilling her action. Heat mushroomed inside her, stopping her breath as effectively as a kick to the solar plexus. She released her lip, unable to stop her mouth from pressing against his thumb.

His strong throat moved on a convulsive swallow. Slowly his thumb stroked her mouth, his eyes fiery and intense. Wanton desire tortured her, weakening her knees, leaving her trembling from head to toe.

Someone moaned. Absently Ana realised it had come from her throat. And somewhere along the way she'd loosened her hold on the robe.

Bastien's gaze slid slowly over her, gleaming, darkening. He uttered something unintelligible in French. His thumb's pressure increased. Ana's lips tingled, heat rushing over her as she gave in to her need and sucked his thumb into her mouth.

'*Non!*' The denial was wrenched from his throat and he stepped back. He swallowed again. 'I will not do this. I will not be like—'

He froze, shoved a hand through his hair before walking stiffly to the door.

'Bastien…?' She stopped, unsure of what to say.

With one hand on the handle, he paused. 'The clothes are yours. Use them. Don't use them. Your choice. But if you wish to ride with me be downstairs in five minutes.'

Ana clutched the bedpost, barely able to stand.

It was happening again. This blind desire, this unstoppable craving that dogged her every time she came within three feet of Bastien. At least he had a handle on his control—enough to stop himself before things went too far.

Whereas she…

Anxiety bit deep at the thought of putting herself in Bastien's presence again so soon. But the fighter in her rebelled at hiding away in her room.

She would borrow the clothes and go for a ride with him. What better way to show him she was as unaffected as he was than by spending a few hours with him without making a fool of herself? Proving that she could control her wayward emotions?

She unzipped the case and found familiar labels neatly stacked. Ana lifted a pair of cream jodhpurs and slid them on, topping it with a camisole and sweater set in chocolate-brown. Black riding boots completed the ensemble, and for the first time in days she felt comfortable. Scraping back her hair into a neat ponytail, she picked up the riding jacket and left her room.

Bastien stood waiting at the bottom of the stairs. 'Tatiana also brought your new contract. Come into my study. You can sign it there.'

Ana frowned 'What new contract?'

'The one that replaces your old one, whose terms you violated. A copy was faxed to your agency yesterday.'

'What…what does it say?' Old and familiar shame crawled up her spine as she followed him down the hall.

'More or less what the old one said. You can read it for yourself. If you're happy with it Chantal will witness it.' He opened the study door and waved her in.

In the large, unashamedly male space, dominated by a huge antique desk, the scent of burning cedarwood drifted from a low fire. But Ana didn't dwell on the charm or the warmth of the room. Her eyes were drawn hypnotically to the document on Bastien's desk.

Her mother's scathing words rushed into her mind.

'You've got your looks. You don't need an education!'

Sliding over the document, Bastien handed her a pen. 'Sign on the last page after you've read it.'

Ana clenched her hand around the pen. 'I won't be rushed, Bastien. I'll sign it once I'm satisfied with it.'

He frowned. 'Organising a shoot on the scale of what the DBH ad needs doesn't happen overnight. Relocating it to another country takes even more time.' His eyes narrowed. 'Are you having second thoughts?'

'No,' she replied hurriedly, her insides churning.

She'd made progress with her disability, but not enough that she could confidently deal with her own paperwork. But the thought of revealing her deficiencies to Bastien made her stomach twist with humiliation.

She glanced down at the paper. Words were jumbled together, morphing into a taunting miasma of black and white that made the document tremble in her hands.

Large, warm hands closed over hers a second before Bastien sank onto his haunches beside her. Startled, she glanced at him. His frown had deepened.

'What's wrong?'

She licked her lips. 'Nothing. I just don't want to rush it in case I miss anything. I…I just need a few minutes. Do you mind getting Chantal?'

His gaze probed hers for several more seconds. Finally he

nodded. His departure brought much needed respite. Desperately she tore through the document, but nothing made sense. Hands shaking, she thrust the contract back onto the desk.

Bastien had faxed a copy to Visual. All she had to do was call and double-check things with Lauren. About to reach for the phone, she stopped when Bastien walked in, followed by Chantal.

'Did you say my agency had approved this?' she asked.

He nodded. 'Yes, I spoke to Lauren this morning.'

Relief coursed through her. Opening the contract to where Bastien had indicated, she carefully signed her name. She felt Bastien's intense gaze on her but refused to glance his way for fear he would see right through her to the heart of her disgrace.

Once the document had been witnessed, Bastien locked it in his drawer and held out his hand to her. 'Now, let's go and visit my horses.'

Pasting a smile on her face, she fell into step beside him.

The morning air was unexpectedly mild, but fresh. Inhaling deeply, she followed Bastien round the side of the château. Landscaped gardens lay to the east, absorbing most of the morning light. She barely had time to admire the profusion of flowers before they came to a large paddock.

Ana spotted the stables just before she caught the whiff of horseflesh. 'How many horses do you own?' she asked.

'I keep six horses here. I have a bigger stable on my estate in Lucerne.'

A tall woman—Chantal's daughter-in-law, she guessed—met them inside the stable. Peering into the semi-darkness, she saw a flash of white. 'Oh, he's magnificent!'

Bastien reached out and patted the horse's nose. 'He is a she. Her name is Storm.'

'What breed?'

'Lipizzaner. From Austria. Slightly smaller than Arabians, but just as swift and powerful.'

Ana leaned forward and stroked Storm's soft nose. 'You're gorgeous. Yes, you are,' she crooned. Her reward was a nudge of approval. She smiled and glanced at Bastien to find his gaze fixed on her.

'She's also very high-spirited, stubborn and reckless. She's thrown more than one rider.'

Something in his voice made her pause. 'Not you, though, right?'

One corner of his mouth tilted up. 'Not me,' he confirmed.

'And what's your secret, pray tell?'

'I've learned to be patient with her—to know when to accommodate her tantrums and when to rein her in.' Stepping forward, he slid a finger between Storm's eyes. 'We've learned to trust each other, but she knows who her master is.'

She couldn't be jealous of a *horse*! And she certainly had no use for all that 'master' nonsense. So why, when Bastien continued to caress Storm, did she experience a pang of envy?

'Come, I'll introduce you to your horse.'

Ana followed, her sense of disquiet increasing as Bastien paused to greet each horse, his voice calm and soothing. Even the fiercest thoroughbred whickered with pleasure.

At the last stall the most beautiful horse she'd ever seen waited. Unlike the other horses, which had shades of grey, this horse was pure white.

'His name is Rebelle,' Bastien said softly. He stroked the animal's neck, then inspected his hooves before instructing the stable hand to saddle him up. His own horse he saddled himself.

They took a path into the woods behind the château, where the smell of earth and dewed vegetation permeated the air. Grasping the reins, Ana tried not to stare at the powerful figure Bastien cut astride his horse, but the wide breadth of his shoulders beneath his tan riding jacket and the powerful thighs that gripped his horse's flanks continually drew her eyes.

Realising she was in danger of losing the task she'd set herself, she cast around in her mind for something to say to ease the tight knot burning in her belly.

Leaning forward, she patted her horse's long neck. 'Does his name mean what I think it does?'

'Rebel? Yes, he arrived prematurely. He was sick and never had a chance to bond with his mother. When she rejected him we thought he wasn't going to make it, but he defied all the odds.'

Inexplicably, a lump lodged in her throat. Ana gave him another pat. 'You'd be amazed how many children make it despite a parent's rejection.'

Too late, she felt Bastien's keen gaze. She held her breath, hoping he wouldn't pick up on her slip. Her hope was dashed.

'You speak from experience.' It was more a statement than a question.

'I'm sure you've guessed Lily isn't exactly the motherly type,' she said breezily, hoping he'd drop the subject.

'How close are you?' he pressed.

'One phone call every three months and a card at Christmas—that close.' Pain darted through her chest and she rubbed at the spot.

He frowned. 'So why does she manage your career?'

'Believe it or not, she's an astute businesswoman when the occasion demands it. As a former model herself, her insight into the business has come in handy on occasion.'

Expecting a censorious reply, she glanced at Bastien and saw him nod thoughtfully.

'Have you been in touch with her lately?'

'She called yesterday to offer advice on how to manage my predicament, as it happens.'

His eyebrows rose. 'And what did that entail?'

'She told me not to get emotionally involved with you.' And for once Ana intended to take her mother's advice.

He drew his horse to a halt. 'And your response was…?' he rasped.

'To say there was little risk of that happening.'

A look crossed his face—part displeasure, part relief. Then he blinked his expression back into neutral. 'Did she offer up any thoughts as who might have planted the drugs?'

Her head snapped up. 'No—why would she?'

'As you said, she has more experience in the modelling world than you do. I'd have thought she'd be fighting to prove your innocence, even if only professionally?'

'Like I said, we don't have the closest relationship. And, no, it's not perfect, but as we both know life rarely ever is.' Digging her heels into Rebelle's side, she set off at a trot.

He caught up with her easily and they rode until they came to a small stream. Dismounting, he took her reins, tied them around a tree and then turned to her. Reading his intention, Ana tried to dismount quickly, but he beat her to it.

He caught her before she could lower herself to the ground. His hands easily encompassed her waist, and the heat of his touch dangerously whittled away her efforts to remain unaffected by him. His scent suffused her senses, his powerful aura closing over her.

'The subject of your mother distresses you,' he said into the still air.

Again that hint of gentleness that threatened to undo her.

She couldn't look at him, so she concentrated on caressing Rebelle's flank. 'Before yesterday I didn't find it easy to admit that she lacks the most fundamental maternal instincts.'

'What happened yesterday?'

'I'm not entirely sure, but she sounded almost…concerned.'

'A child's hope is a very tough thing to kill.'

'Are you speaking of you or me?'

His mouth pursed. 'Mine died a long time ago.'

A harsh laugh escaped her. 'Are you sure? Sometimes the heart wants what the heart wants.'

He stilled completely. Ana could almost hear him clinically analysing her words. 'Then perhaps you should listen to your head and not your heart.'

Unable to stop herself, she turned and looked into his eyes. 'Is that what you do? Shut off your feelings whenever it suits you?'

His hand tightened, albeit imperceptibly. 'I feel. I just don't let blind emotion get in the way of my better judgement.'

'Then *bravo* to you.' She forced a teasing tone. 'And I to-tally get the feeling that blind emotion wouldn't try to get in your way. It would run screaming in the other direction when it saw you coming.'

'I can live with that.'

She frowned at his bleak tone and glanced up to see a wave of pain wash over his face before his expression blanked again.

A wave of sadness surged out of nowhere. 'Bastien, are you okay?'

His mouth twisted in a parody of a smile. 'Of course. Come. There's a view I want to show you.'

His breath whispered over her ear, his low voice a deep rum-ble over her sensitive nerve-endings.

She followed him through a tall stand of birches, trying to take pleasure in birdsong and warm sunshine. But all she could think of was Bastien's expression and his bleak reply.

His long strides carried them along a narrow path to a small clearing where the trees ended on a wide natural ledge cut into the hillside. Moving alongside him, Ana took a stunned breath. The valley was spread out in picture-perfection below her. The view extended all way to the lake, with the château a golden vi-sion amongst the rolling green. Dazzling in the morning light, with nothing around for miles, it resembled something out of a child's fairytale. Or a woman's dream come true.

Beside her, Bastien took a deep breath, a look almost of con-tentment on his face.

'Why did you bring me here?' she asked.

He shrugged. 'I thought you might want to see it.' His gaze met hers briefly before he looked away.

'The château has stunning views at every turn. But this is your favourite view, isn't it?' she asked intuitively.

He smiled. 'Yes,' he said simply.

Something warm, soft, unfurled in her chest…she was inor-dinately pleased that he'd shared this moment with her.

She pointed to a summit in the distance. 'What are those peaks? They look like…'

'Horns? They're called Les Diablerets—the devil's horns.'

Ana grinned. 'Very apt. Thanks for showing me this view. I think it would make a stunning backdrop for the shoot.'

His face blanked, his smile disappearing. 'The shoot?' he repeated coolly.

She gestured to the landscape. 'Yes, the castle in Scotland was beautiful, but this is absolutely breathtaking. I think it's perfect, actually.'

'Of course,' he intoned, his voice flat.

Ana glanced at him and her smile faltered. 'It was your idea to relocate the shoot here, Bastien.'

'I'm aware of that.'

'Then why do I feel I've just stepped on a landmine by referring to it?'

His jaw clenched. '*C'est rien.* It's nothing.' He turned and headed back to the horses. He helped her up, handed over her reins, then mounted his horse.

Thick silence cloaked them until she couldn't stand it any more.

'Did you grow up here?'

At first she thought he wouldn't answer. Then he nodded. 'When my grandfather bought the château it was in ruins. He restored it brick by brick and lived here his whole life. My father kept it because it was close to the city.'

'Not because of its sentimental value?' Ana joked, secretly wishing back the smile she'd glimpsed on the hilltop.

His face remained impassive. 'Sentiment has little place in business in the twenty-first century.'

'So why do you keep it, then?'

Her question seemed to surprise him. 'It's a good investment.'

'Emotionally or financially?'

Cool grey eyes fastened on her. His horse, sensing his altered mood, whickered anxiously. 'Don't try to psychoanalyse me, Ana,' he warned softly.

'Because you're such an enigma?'

His eyes glittered. 'On the contrary, I'm a very simple man. I know what I want. I also know when the price is too high for me to pay. I cannot afford you, Ana Duval.'

With a kick of his horse's flanks, he surged forward.

She caught up with him at the stables. 'What did you mean by that?'

They both dismounted and he took her reins and stared down at her. 'You live your life in unabashed emotion. Unbridled passion is great in the bedroom, but in the real world all it does is let you down. I prefer not to become embroiled in the inevitable messy aftermath. Once was enough.'

'Since I don't recall offering myself to you on a silver platter, I'm assuming your ego is once again in full residence? Or are you just too scared to take a chance on feeling anything other than bitterness for the rest of your life because your belief in love and happiness was shattered once?'

He inhaled sharply. 'Love? Don't confuse love with sex or duty, Ana. Sex has a limited shelf-life and duty is very easy to shirk when it becomes too burdensome.'

His face contorted into a mask of pain before he exhaled and blinked it away. But that wasn't before her heart lurched at the stark insight into Bastien's beliefs.

'Bastien—'

'Chantal will have breakfast ready. Go ahead. I'll meet you in the dining room shortly.'

The content, smiling Bastien from the hilltop had disappeared. Impassive, corporate Bastien was back, his face giving nothing away as he led the horses off.

Ana walked slowly back to the château, Bastien's words haunting her. Their bleakness lodged a thorn in her heart. Had the events of sixteen years ago affected him so much that he'd shut off his heart completely?

Wrenching the tie from her ponytail, she speared her fingers through her hair. She had no business feeling sorry for Bastien.

Feeling sorry for the fact that he wouldn't let himself feel, or want, or need. And she absolutely had no business wishing he would feel for her, or want or even need her.

CHAPTER SEVEN

BASTIEN PUT THE phone down and scrubbed a hand over his face. Three days and his investigators had come up empty. Whoever had framed Ana had covered their tracks very well. The police had reported no fingerprints on the inhaler. Not even Ana's…

He frowned.

He'd seen first-hand the extraordinary measures to which people would go to gain wealth and power. How ruthless and determined people could be.

Sixteen years ago Lily Duval had set her deadly sights on his father and employed an almost obsessive single-mindedness in order to seduce him away from his wife and rip his family apart.

And she'd succeeded. That last day in Verbier was for ever etched in his memory—and not just because of his mother's blotched, tearstained face as she'd pleaded with his father, nor the roar of his father's car as he'd driven off, a triumphant Lily Duval by his side.

It was the day his parents had rejected him completely. The day he'd learned to shut off his emotions once and for all.

The silence especially was what he remembered most. He'd retreated to the icy-cold gazebo, his sanctuary, where he'd known no one would disturb him. He wasn't sure how much time had passed and then he'd heard his father's hoarse, frantic call. Seen his ashen face. Watched Lily Duval's manic rage as she'd seen the life she'd almost attained disappearing.

Ana's serene composure had been most shocking of all. She

hadn't even blinked when she'd been been instructed to fetch her things. As if she was used to it...

The library door opened, wrenching him from his thoughts.

Ana saw him and faltered. 'Oh, I thought you were in your study—' She turned to leave, her willowy figure silhouetted perfectly in the hallway light.

He'd relocated to the library because of her. The layout of the château had never troubled him until he'd heard her speaking to her father in Spanish in the sitting room next to his study, her smoky voice hypnotic...enthralling.

Although aware she was half-Colombian, he knew very little about that side of her heritage. Hearing her speak the foreign tongue, the unmistakable excitement in her voice, had made him lose concentration more than once.

'Come in. I need to talk to you.'

Her trepidation as she stepped into the room grated. Was he *that* unapproachable?

She sat and crossed her legs, and he tried not to let his gaze drop. He failed. Her long, shapely legs, bare and lightly tanned despite the time of year, made Bastien's blood rush a little faster through his veins.

Get a grip!

He picked up the file on his desk. 'My investigators have drawn a blank.'

Her eyes widened. When she bit her lip, Bastien forced himself not to groan.

'They found nothing at all?'

'It seems not.'

A look flitted across her face, one she tried hard to mask. Bastien's suspicions prickled.

'One thing puzzled me, though.'

Her wary gaze shot to his. 'What?'

'The police found no fingerprints on the inhaler. Not even yours.'

She shot up out of her chair, the movement causing her breasts to bounce. His hand tightened on the file.

'What does that mean? You don't still think I'm lying about this, do you?'

The hurt in her voice caught him on the raw.

'Calm down. I didn't say that. What aren't you telling me, Ana?'

Her face remained carefully neutral. 'I'm not following you.'

He sat back in his chair. 'You're holding something back. I don't want to think the worst—'

'But you're going to anyway.'

He shrugged. 'We both know how irrational women and men can be when they're fixated on something.'

She paled and sank back into her chair. Bastien's earlier niggle of doubt returned…expanded.

'Let me get this straight. You think I'm fixated on you?' she whispered.

'It's not beyond the realms of possibility.'

One shapely brow arched. 'Really? Is there an app for that? Because I'd like to have one for Christmas.'

His jaw clenched. 'Don't get flippant with me, Ana.'

'And don't get too far up yourself, Bastien, or you might trip and break your neck. Need I remind you that everything that's happened between us so far has been mutual?' she threw at him, then surged out of her seat and headed for the door.

He was up and blocking her way before he'd even realised what he was doing. 'This conversation isn't over.'

'Yes, it is. To think I deluded myself into believing I was wrong about you. That you would be interested in helping me.'

She reached past him. He stayed her by taking her arm. Smooth skin registered beneath his fingers, her firm muscles clenching in resistance.

'Ana, stop.'

'Go to hell!' she snapped, then mauled at her lip again.

That single action caused his blood to boil, to pool somewhere decidedly south. This time he didn't want to still the movement with his hand. He wanted to use his mouth.

'You're biting your lip again. Something's up.'

Her sigh released her trapped flesh. 'You credit me with too much guile, Bastien. Trust me—I'm not worthy of it.'

'Too late. I know just how beguiling and bewitching you can be when it suits you.'

Her slap came swift and hard. It stung. It also brought him alive in ways Bastien had never imagined. Within seconds he was hard, his erection strong and unstoppable. The hoarse, shaken sound that had emitted from her throat brought his attention to her sleek neck, to the frantic hammering pulse.

Without stopping to think, he lowered his head and flicked his tongue against it. Her shocked gasp washed over his jaw. Drawing her closer, he closed his mouth over her pulse, needing to connect with her life force.

'No.'

Her protest was firm and solid—nothing like the debilitating weakness that flooded him.

He paused. Slowly he raised his head. Her eyes were pools of hurt, wide and aching. The vice in his chest tightened. When her lips worked as if she wanted to say more his gaze fell to her moist, plump mouth. It tempted him…a siren's call he couldn't resist.

With a suppressed groan, he started to lower his head again.

'No,' she stressed again. 'I'm not fixated on you, Bastien.'

The words were said with a conviction that stopped his breath. But he wanted her to be. Just as he was fixated on her. She'd already succeeded in getting under his skin. She made him want everything he shouldn't.

Hell, last night he'd even found himself reaching for the phone. He'd been halfway to dialling his mother's cell phone before he'd stopped himself. Knowing she was responsible for him placing himself in a position of possible rejection should have made him angry. Instead something had shifted inside him, and the instincts that had seen him through some tough and tricky times had urged him down a different path. A shaky, unsettling path of *maybe* and…*hope*.

'What aren't you telling me, Ana? If you want me to help you, talk to me.'

His breath stalled as he waited for her to answer.

Her eyes slid from his, distress evident in her face. 'I… I've been wondering if my mother has anything to do with the drugs…'

Her gaze clashed with his for a fleeting second, then slid away again. But in that split moment he glimpsed deep hurt in their soulful depths.

Bastien realised how difficult it had been for her to admit that. And how brave. He cupped her face in his hands. The pulse of arousal still throbbed in his blood but an underlying tenderness rose out of nowhere—an urge to comfort her that swamped him, left him unable to breathe. He wanted to step back, to withdraw from the feeling, but he found he couldn't move. Found his hands gentling, his head dipping so he could look into her eyes.

'Why do you think it was her?' he asked softly.

Her breath shuddered out. 'She was fired from her job. She gets mean when she's upset, but after our conversation yesterday I'm not so sure…' She choked to a halt.

'I'll have the investigators look into it.'

Her gaze anxiously searched his. 'What if I'm wrong? I know you think I'm foolish, but if there's hope for our relationship I don't want to ruin it.'

Knowing the emotion he'd let himself entertain, how could he condemn her? 'You're not foolish. And I'll make sure it's kept discreet.'

Her smile bloomed, lighting up her face. Lighting up inside him. Again something tightened in his chest—harder this time.

The ground shifted beneath his feet.

He wanted to block out her voice by whatever means necessary, to throw caution to the wind, sweep her into his arms and carry her to his bed. His gut tightened as every sense clamoured for just one more taste of her sensual lips. For a chance to cup her breasts, bury his face between them as he surged inside her.

She was casting a spell over him. He knew that. And yet he couldn't move away.

'Thank you. Sorry I slapped you,' she tagged on, but a small smile teased her lips.

'Why do I get the impression you don't really mean that?'

Her smile grew. 'Because you've got a very suspicious mind?'

'Maybe, but my instincts still warn me that you're dangerous to me, Ana Duval.' The words spilled out before he could stop them.

Her eyes widened. She gave a shocked laugh. 'I'm not *dangerous*.'

With a twist of his body he reversed their places, backed her against the door. 'Then why do I feel as if I have to have you or lose my mind?'

Heat blossomed in her cheeks. 'You—you do?'

'I want… I *need* to make love with you. You're like a fever in my blood. Last I heard a fever not broken can kill. Which makes you a serious threat to my life.'

Ana couldn't tear her gaze from Bastien's face. His words wove a dangerous spell over her. A spell she wanted to throw herself into wholeheartedly.

Her mind spun, unable to keep a firm hold on reality.

'You don't mean that.' Her words emerged from a throat thick with desire.

He pressed his body against hers. 'I do. You're in my head, in my blood…'

She couldn't deny the powerful message from his body. He wanted her. And, as much as she wanted to deny it, she wanted him too. Badly.

And that was insanity itself…

His head descended again.

One kiss. Just one kiss and then you'll stop, a tiny voice whispered.

Only it was less of a kiss and more of a possession.

Bastien took control of her mouth and ravaged her senses. His hands cupped her breasts and she moaned, her craving intensifying. What he was doing wasn't enough. She wanted more—much more. She wanted no barriers between them, wanted his hands on her, skin to skin.

As if he'd heard her silent plea he dropped his hands to the seam of her top and pulled it up. Firm hands caressed her bare midriff, forcing her breath out of her lungs. Blood surged underneath her skin, escalating the dizzy spin already sending her off course.

Hanging on to the belief that she was in control, that she could stop despite the haziness of her thoughts, she thrust her tongue against his, savouring its rough texture and boldly following it when Bastien retreated. His chest lifted, sucking in air. His grip tightened at her waist, and then he was easing her top higher, his intent clear.

Ana briefly considered protesting but the fever raging through her was all-consuming—a powerful drug more potent than the heroin she'd been accused of taking. The whisper of air over her skin barely registered before Bastien drew her closer once more. His heat scorched her. He touched, caressed, coaxed the very fire from the core of her being as his hands trailed over her skin.

A sense of awakening overwhelmed Ana. Tears prickled behind her closed lids and she fought to breathe as sensation bombarded her. And through it all Bastien continued to ravage her lips as if he couldn't get enough.

'Touch me,' he commanded hoarsely.

She obeyed.

His muscles clenched at the touch of her hands on his back. Tentative, excited, she caressed him, following the sleek, toned power of his shoulders until her hands settled on his nape. A deep groan rumbled from his chest, the sound evoking a well of pleasure inside her.

Clenching a fist in his hair, she tugged his head down, bolder in the effort to wring one last ounce of pleasure from the kiss. Because she had to stop soon…had to—

He bit her lower lip as he pinched her hardened nipples. Ana cried out. Liquid fire pooled between her thighs, drenching her with need.

He lifted his head and stared down at her, eyes stormy grey with barely leashed passion. Deliberately, he moulded her breasts, his action slow, tormenting. Another hoarse gasp echoed through the room. Without breaking eye contact he pulled down her bra cup and sucked one hardened nipple into his mouth.

Ana watched, and the sight was so erotic, her knees buckled.

With every pass of his tongue he drove her closer to an unfamiliar precipice. Her fingers tightened in his hair and she was unable to look away as he performed magic with his tongue. He squeezed her breasts together, his movements urgent.

Just when she thought it couldn't get any more delicious he straightened and reached for her bra clasp.

'I need to see you.'

Her instincts screeched, belatedly swamping her with a sense of preservation. 'No…'

'*Oui,*' he stressed, the untamed glint in his eyes drying her mouth.

'I can't. God, you don't even *like* me!'

He tensed, his face registering surprise. 'That's not true. You can't help who you are—'

Her shocked laughter cut off his words. Roughly, she pushed him away. 'I can't believe you insult me in one breath and want to make love to me in another.'

He shook his head. 'You misunderstand. Lust isn't logical.' One hand speared through his hair, mussing the dark gold strands. 'Whether we like each other or not, we can't help the way we feel, *ma belle*. The chemistry between us isn't rational, but it's there—undeniable. Maybe this is one way to get rid of it.'

'You mean get it out of our systems?' She couldn't believe she was half-naked, having this conversation with Bastien.

He shrugged again. 'Why not?'

'Because it would make us no better than rutting animals!'

He cupped her jaw, his thumb caressing her skin before tilting her face to his. 'And how long do you think we can keep avoiding it until it ravages us?'

She licked her lips, desire drowning her even as she fought to stay sane. 'We don't have to give in to our impulses just because the urge is there.'

He gave a low, husky laugh. 'Really?'

Slowly, deliberately, he lowered his head. His lips brushed hers once. Twice. She moaned. Another laugh, another kiss. Light, ephemeral. Fresh tingles shot down her spine, singeing every cell until she was engulfed in sensual flames.

'Then walk away,' Bastien commanded, his mouth a hairsbreadth from hers.

'Wh—what?'

'Prove we're not animals. Walk away. If you can.' His thumb performed another pass, then rested on her frantic pulse.

'Bastien…' she protested. Feebly.

'I won't stop you if you want to end this. But do you want to deny yourself this exquisite pleasure?'

'I…' She couldn't conjure up more than that single word.

'By morning we will have dealt with it. Then we simply return to the way things were, minus the desperate need to tear each other's clothes off.'

Ana opened her mouth to refuse. Her lips brushed his. She tried to pull away. He stayed her with a firm touch. But reality had intruded enough for her to know that accepting his offer would be madness, tantamount to retracting every vow she'd made to herself.

The harsh consequences of her mother's promiscuity warned her against giving in to her baser instincts, against surrendering to this heady, insatiable need to satisfy the craving that tore at her soul. No matter how painful.

She shook her head.

Bastien's chest expanded on a deep, slow breath. There was a mildly stunned look in his eyes. Then he released her.

Ana felt as if part of her had been ripped out. He was walking away. The thought tore a jagged path through her mind, bringing with it the knowledge that cracked open a belief she'd never contemplated.

She wasn't her mother. Which meant she could take what she wanted and not destroy anything or anyone in the process.

She wasn't stringing anyone along or making false promises.

There was a finite outcome to this. Bastien had offered the perfect solution. She could take this unique journey with this man who set her world on fire, explore what promised to be untold pleasure, and still keep her dignity and her heart intact.

Deep in her heart Ana knew she'd never experience this level of chemistry with another man. Bastien was the only man who'd ever elicited such riotous, incredible feelings within her. What if this was her only chance of pleasure at its headiest? Could she deny herself this?

His expression shuttering, he started to turn away. She grabbed his hand and returned it to her cheek.

Fierce eyes, demanding and powerful, locked on hers. 'Ana?'

Turning her head, she kissed his palm. 'Yes.'

His nose flared. 'There's no going back from here. You have to know this.' His voice emerged thick and deep.

She swallowed. 'I do.'

One arm snagged her waist and lifted her away from the door. Before she could form another word he swung her into his arms, entered the hallway and strode for the stairs.

She buried her face in his neck, breathed in his potent smell and tried to stem the flicker of apprehension inside her.

In his room, he lowered her to her feet and eased off her top. His hands slid up into her hair to tilt her face to his. 'You're beautiful,' he stated simply.

Ana cleared her throat, aware that she needed to warn him about her inexperience before it was too late. 'Bastien, there's something you should know. I'm not… I don't do this lightly.'

He dropped a long, sensual kiss on her mouth. '*Oui*, I know. It is why I will make this special for you,' he rasped, his gaze devouring her as he reached behind her and slowly unzipped her skirt.

His gaze didn't stray from her face as the material pooled at her feet. Nevertheless Ana's body flamed. She felt more naked than she ever had in her life.

Desperately, she cleared her throat. 'I don't mean that.' She licked her lips, frantic for the right words to explain what she meant. 'I mean my experience is somewhat limited.' She couldn't bear it if he were disappointed.

He paused, his chest expanding on a breath. 'Ana, I'm almost at breaking point. So are you. Now is not the time to apprise me of your experiences—limited or otherwise.'

'But there isn't—'

He hooked his T-shirt over his head, ripped down his trousers and boxers, and stood naked before her.

Ana had never seen a more gorgeous specimen of man. And that was saying a lot, considering her profession. Bastien's body was more than an extraordinary streamlined symmetry of flesh and bone. It was fluid, lithe, and graceful in ways she could never accurately describe. And most of all he was proudly masculine and unashamed of it.

His erection throbbed with a life of its own. She stared, unable to look away, as he advanced and captured her in his arms.

'If you insist on talking,' he rasped, before seizing her mouth in another searing kiss, 'tell me your favourite position, *ma petite*. We'll start with that.'

Shocked laughter tripped from her. 'My favourite...?' She couldn't repeat his question—nor could she stop the fierce blush that suffused her face. 'Ah, *Dios*!'

He traced a finger over her cheek. 'I'm not sure which turns me on harder—hearing you speak in Spanish or your blushes,' he said huskily, lowering his head to graze hot lips over her skin.

Continuing along her jaw, he slowly circled her until he stood behind her. Scooping her hair into one hand, he trailed kisses along her shoulders.

Ana shivered uncontrollably, her temperature spiking to dangerous levels. She fought to stay upright as he traced a breath-stealing erotic path over her skin. Eyes drifting shut, she reached out and grasped the bedpost, harsh pants of need exploding from her chest as she succumbed to the wonder of sensations buffeting her.

At the base of her spine he lingered, flicked his tongue against her skin just above her panty line. He grasped her hips, his strong hold stamping his desire on her, and turned her to face him.

Opening her eyes, she stared down into stormy grey eyes. His skin was flushed, his face stark with barely controlled desire. At the back of her mind Ana registered that he seemed as affected by the roiling sensation as she was, but the thought was fleeting. Because she read his intent and every muscle clenched tight.

'No!'

He paused, his sensual mouth so close to the wet evidence of her arousal. 'You don't like the idea of my mouth on you?'

She shook her head, shivering when her hair brushed over sensitised nipples. 'It's not that. It's just… I've never…'

His eyes registered surprise, then morphed into a calculating, anticipatory gleam. 'If you've *never*, then how do you know you don't like it?'

'Bastien, *por favor*—oh!'

Shoving aside her thong, he placed an open-mouthed kiss on her, his tongue darting out to lick in bold sweeps. Sensation rocked her, completely sapping her strength. She collapsed onto the bed, helped in no small measure by Bastien's firm push. She cried out, her back arching off the bed as he suckled.

Ana should have felt ashamed—embarrassed at the wanton, pagan pleasure she was taking in the act being performed on her. But sheer bliss beyond her imagining had taken over. Her thighs fell apart and Bastien moved between them, his body surging closer as he continued to create magic between her legs.

Her flesh tingled, tightened with minute, unfamiliar spasms that shortened her already depleted breath. The intensity of her reaction stunned her into screaming.

The sound spurred Bastien on. He laid his mouth against her, teasing the ultra-sensitive place that finally sent her over the edge. She was vaguely aware of thrashing on the bed, unable to stop the fierce waves of ecstasy rolling through her, or to stop her fists from pounding against the sheets as she broke free and crashed in a blaze of fiery wonder.

Gentle hands soothed her, brought her slowly back to reality. Opening her eyes, she encountered Bastien's smouldering gaze. She was lying against the pillows, both legs trapped underneath his more powerful, hair-roughened one. He leaned on one elbow and with his free hand reached up to caress the damp hair away from her temple.

'You're so incredibly responsive, *ma petite*,' he husked out, his voice sandpaper-rough.

'That unbridled passion you hate?'

'That unbridled passion I don't mind so much in bed. Perhaps even a little bit out of it.'

He swooped and devoured her gasp. He cradled her skull, imprisoning her, all the better to ravage her lips. Fresh, potent arrows of lust shot through her, invigorating her lulled senses, bringing them back to life. Her moan was smothered beneath their frenzied kiss. Her hands settled on the firm skin of his back. The need to feel every inch of him was a powerful urge tripping through her.

Bastien made a sound: half-growl, half-encouragement. She traced the skin on the small of his back. When he moaned again she ventured lower, clasped his taut buttocks.

It was only when he reared over her, settled his powerful frame over her, that Ana realised her panties were missing. Bastien's thick arousal nudged against her, its hot, potent force sending a momentary pang of anxiety spiking through her.

Sensing it immediately, Bastien eased his mouth from hers and gazed down at her. 'You need not worry, Ana. Trust me. I won't hurt you.'

Something melted deep inside her. She exhaled shakily, unable to utter a word past the emotional lump in her throat. Reaching up, she threaded her fingers through the lock of hair that had fallen over his brow.

Bastien kissed his way down her cleavage, changed direction to slowly circle one breast. Waiting for him to reach the hard pinnacle brought its own torture. But finally he took one nipple in his mouth. Her eyes fluttered shut and she gave herself over to her feelings. She touched him everywhere, including that utterly gorgeous hard erection. Her exploration was short-lived when he soon removed her hand and kissed the back of it.

The sight of him sheathing himself flooded her with renewed need.

Slowly Bastien lowered himself over her, his gaze capturing hers as he nudged her entrance. Tension, excruciating and urgent, flowed between them, feeding the heady anticipation of their union. A strangled moan escaped her throat as he probed deeper. Her fingers tingled, fluttered closer to hold him. Capturing her hand, he imprisoned it above her head. The thrill of semi-freedom sent a bolt of pleasure through her. With her free hand she clasped his buttock.

He responded by surging into her.

Her wince coincided with his gasp of disbelief.

Ana tried to keep her face blank as his gaze searched hers, but she knew he'd caught her reaction. She closed her eyes as he froze.

'Ana, look at me,' he demanded hoarsely.

She lifted her gaze. She'd been expecting disappointment, maybe censure. But she encountered a blistering gaze filled with a hunger that stopped her breath.

'You're beautiful. Incredible,' he said simply.

The words broke something free inside her. Instinctively she moved, sliding her inner muscles along his rigid length.

A heartfelt groan rumbled through his chest. Acclimatising to the reactions of her body, she moved again, shuddering with the pleasure that came with the minute action. Bastien clasped her hips, stilled her.

For endless moments he remained still. Then with a harsh groan he surged deeper. Ecstasy rolled through her. Eagerly she awaited his next thrust, her heart pounding when it arrived, more incredible than the last.

All too soon the tingling began—fiercer, sharper than before. When it swept her away Ana knew she'd only experienced a fraction of pleasure the first time. Hoarse cries seared her throat as she soared higher and higher.

Bastien plunged deeper, his movements frantic, his skin sweat-slicked as he dipped his head to kiss her. She responded with fervour, her senses clamouring to give him as much satisfaction as he'd given her.

Their tongues met and he groaned deeply. With one last surge he tensed, freezing for a moment in time before a series of convulsions shook his frame.

Ana clasped him to her, her chest meeting his hot, damp skin as he settled on her. Against her heart she felt his thunder wildly, echoing her own's chaotic beat.

Tu es perfecto.

She wasn't sure whether she'd said the words aloud. She didn't care. She felt too replete, too sated. Her eyelids fluttered, drifted down. She tried to fight sleep, managed a feeble protest when Bastien dropped a kiss on the corner of her mouth and left the bed. But it was no use.

And Ana's last thought before sleep claimed her was that her life would never be the same again.

CHAPTER EIGHT

HE'D PULLED THE sheet over her when he'd left the bed but now one foot had escaped. Its delicate arch teased him, taunted him with a want he'd hoped to ease by now.

Bastien stared at it, willed himself not to reach for it.

Focus!

There were important things to work through, figure out. He needed to leave, to return to his own bedroom.

You're in your own bedroom.

Hell, he was losing it. His jaw clenched tight.

Since he'd stepped foot inside that courtroom and seen Ana again everything had fallen off-kilter. He was being buffeted by emotions he didn't know what to do with.

His brain especially seemed to be playing tricks on him. Otherwise why would he have imagined Ana's virginity? And why would the thought have sent such a thrill through him? Why would he be perched on the edge of the bed now, watching her sleep, wishing he could wake her up and experience their incredibly exhilarating lovemaking over and over again?

He shoved a hand through his hair and started to rise.

She stirred, lazily stretching, tempting the sheet down a little further. Fire roared through his veins. He had to get out of here. There were several guestrooms where he could spend the rest of the night.

Seductive eyes opened, focused on him. 'Is it still night?'

'Yes.' He steeled himself against the exquisitely languorous look in her eyes and madly scrambled for something to say. 'How long have you been celibate?' He hadn't meant to ask that, but the words spilled out anyway.

She sat up slowly, pulling the sheet to cover her breasts. He curbed the urge to rip it away, feast his eyes on her—

'My whole life,' she answered.

He froze. 'You were a virgin?'

The thought confused, astounded...*pleased* him? He pushed the last feeling away, but it kept returning.

'Yes.'

He'd been her first. 'Why didn't you tell me?' Why did his voice sound so damned hoarse?

'What difference would it have made?'

Her voice was sleep-husky, her hair spilling in bed-tumbled disarray over her naked shoulders. The sight of the white sheet against her tanned skin did incredible things to his libido.

He felt himself slipping under her spell again. Confusion mingled with lust and self-loathing sent him to his feet. 'A hell of a lot!'

'I tried to tell you—'

'You didn't try hard enough!'

'But you knew...you must have realised...'

His mind raced. He'd been eager, uncouth. Like a wolf during mating season, his need had come second to none. He'd been the animal she'd accused him of being. All he'd wanted was to trap her underneath him, feast on her softness and incredible responsiveness. Nothing else had mattered but having her.

Not even the fact that she'd been a virgin.

He sank onto the bed, his thigh tantalisingly close to that tempting foot. He swallowed as fire shot through his pelvis.

'Bastien, no one held a gun to your head. You could have stopped any time you wanted.'

The truth of the statement shamed him even more. 'No, I'm afraid I couldn't have.' Because he'd been too far gone to stop. 'But if you'd told me things would've been different.'

She licked her lips, sending his heart-rate rocketing. *Mon*

Dieu, he had to find some distance or this thing happening between them would consume him whole.

Her foot flexed.

'How different?' she husked out.

'I would've been gentler, taken more time and care.'

You still could... The thought teased the fringes of his mind. Possibilities tantalised.

Before he could stop himself he reached out and grabbed her foot.

Her breath caught and her foot arched into his touch. 'I'm glad you didn't. Any slower and one of us would've resorted to violence.'

Reluctantly, his lips twitched. Moving closer, he lifted her foot into his lap. Slowly he massaged her soft skin, fascinated by her tiny gasps of pleasure at his simple caress. The sheet slipped lower. With a firm tug he pulled it away.

She blushed. Unbidden, their conversation on the tarmac replayed in his mind, now taking on a different meaning. Her blushes weren't a clever tool to entice a man. She blushed because she was genuinely innocent.

The thought shocked him into stillness. Questions tumbled through his mind and assumptions disintegrated, fuelling his confusion. She wasn't the wanton seductress he'd thought her to be. She had been a virgin.

He had no right to be here with her.

As if diametrically opposed to the idea, his hand tightened around her ankle.

She responded by flexing her foot directly into his groin.

'*Mon Dieu*, Ana.' Desire, fierce and hot, pulsed through him with an urgency that stopped every other thought. His gaze rose along with his temperature, moved over the smooth suppleness of her calf, her pale golden thighs, to the wet glistening of her sex nestling between the triangle of carefully groomed hair. He paused there, heady satisfaction settling inside him at the thought that he'd been her first.

As if reacting to the heat of his gaze, a delicate shudder raked her frame.

His scrutiny continued upward. Over her flat stomach up to the soft mounds of her breasts. The sight of her nipples fuelled his need to taste them again. Her chest rose and fell with short, frantic pants that set his own heart thundering. Her swollen lips parted, her pink tongue resting against them.

When his eyes finally captured hers it was the look in the chocolate depths that floored him. Daring, innocent anticipation. Need. A heady combination that had him discarding her foot along with his intention to leave her be and search out a different bed for the night.

He'd promised himself one night, after all. He'd stick to that promise. By morning he should be rid of this insane, inexplicable desire for Ana Duval. Once he had it bottled and shelved he could rest easier.

Rearing over her, he kissed her. She parted for him immediately, her tongue searching out his with a newly gained confidence that threatened to blow him away. She was learning fast, his Ana.

No. She wasn't his Ana. She was just his for the night.

The thought sent a strange bolt of displeasure through him, but not enough to stop him from groaning his satisfaction as her hands closed over his back, her fingers beginning a delicate caressing of his flesh that sent blood surging into his groin.

He was so ready, so tortuously aroused, he feared he'd explode any second. Pulling back from the kiss to give himself a little breathing room, he dropped light kisses on her jaw, her delicate earlobe.

And still she continued to wreak havoc with her fingers. In desperation Bastien plucked another condom from the bedside table and slipped it on. He'd promised her it would be different this time, but he wasn't so sure he could keep that promise.

But he would try even if it killed him.

'Turn over.' At least if he wasn't looking into her achingly beautiful face or dreaming of kissing her senseless he might be able to pull back from the brink of this insanity that engulfed him.

'What?' Even hesitant, her voice hitched, filled with an anticipation that didn't help his control one little bit.

Except the thought of making love to her like this was even headier than taking her missionary-style. He cursed under his breath. He'd started this. He aimed to finish it.

He lifted a forefinger and slowly rotated it. Eyes wide, alluring beyond measure, she reversed her position.

If he'd hoped for a little reprieve he was sorely disappointed. Her back—slim, smooth and faintly indented with her delicate spine—taunted him. It dipped to her impossibly small waist before flaring to accommodate feminine hips and a firm, rounded behind.

Everything about her was elegantly feminine, intensely seductive—especially the way she caught and pulled her hair over one shoulder so she could watch him watching her.

He bent forward, placed his lips on her first vertebrae. Another delicate shudder racked her body. He kissed his way down, determined not to drown in her moans of pleasure. He reached her waist and spanned it with his hands, glorying in the velvety warmth of her skin as his tongue dipped into the faint dimples just above her buttocks.

'Bastien…'

His name had never sounded so arousing. He sucked in a fortifying breath and closed his eyes to restore a little sanity. When he glanced up, her gaze was locked on his.

She was ready. He was more than fit to burst. With one kiss deposited on each globe of her rear, he kissed his way up her spine.

He settled them on the bed, her back to his front. Reaching an arm around her, he lifted her leg and pulled it back over his hip. This time when she turned to look at him he was ready for her. He planted a hot, hungry kiss on her soft ruby-coloured mouth.

'This is my favourite position. Tell me if you like it.'

He thrust inside her, giving a muted sound of pleasure when

her tight inner muscles closed around him. One hand on her stomach held her firm as he thrust again.

She cried out, sending his senses spiralling higher.

'Do you like it?' He had to know—had to hear her say it.

'Yes.' The word was dragged out of her. It echoed through the room and infused him with a satisfaction he'd never craved before. Spearing a hand through her hair, he held her, kissed her as his hips rocked back and forth.

Her arm curved over the back of his head as if to hold him. *I'm not going anywhere. You're mine.* The words filtered through his subconscious. Their deeper meaning threatened to invade his mind, but it splintered apart with the force of his desire.

Ana tore her lips from his, her breath fracturing as she neared her peak. He caught a delicate earlobe between his lips, his own need clamouring for release. Minute spasms caressed his shaft. He groaned, watched her eyes flutter closed as her bottom pushed forcefully against his pelvis.

'Bastien!' She grasped his arm, convulsions raking through her as she gave in to her climax.

With a roar that drowned out her cries he thrust one last time. He came with a rush that emptied every last coherent thought from his mind, leaving him free to soar as he'd never soared before.

At the back of his mind he knew he held her too tightly, that he risked bruising her soft skin, but he needed to hold on because she represented the only safe thing to hang on to as he experienced an unprecedented level of pleasure.

Bastien told himself it was impossible, that he was merely imagining it, but he closed his eyes, unwilling to confront his feelings as spasms continued to rake his body.

When they finally subsided he dropped one last, spent kiss on her jaw. Words, unfamiliar and unnerving, trembled on the edges of his mind.

'You were *magnifique, ma petite,*' he croaked. He wanted

to say more, but he stopped himself just in time. He was already way out of his comfort zone.

Ana came awake slowly. Which should have warned her that something was different. Normally she awoke instantly, her mind fresh, alert.

It was almost as if her subconscious wanted to protect her from the harsh reality of the morning after.

She knew immediately she was alone.

His scent clung to the sheets. She steeled herself not to bury her face in the pillow, breathe deeply and imprint his potent smell on her senses for all time.

He'd kept his word.

One night only. The fact that he hadn't stuck around till morning caused her heart to shrivel with pain. He'd slept with her and now he was done with her.

Remembering their lovemaking—how wanton and needy she'd been—brought a rush of heat to her cheeks. That last time, just as dawn had broken, she'd thought she'd die with pleasure…had even lost touch with reality for several seconds.

Was this what drove her mother? Why she chased after men with such relentless purpose? If this feeling was what she experienced every time she found a new man then Ana could understand a small measure of why her mother did what she did.

Ana's every sinew sang with fulfilment even though she knew she'd never relive this experience again.

The knowledge shortened her breath, lodged fear deep in her heart, making her fiercely glad Bastien wasn't around. She had a hard enough time hiding her feelings from him normally. Raw and naked like this he would have spotted her turmoil in seconds. Every single promise she'd made to stay away from him had come to nothing. In the end she'd fallen into his arm with damning ease.

She shifted and immediately her body reminded her of last night. She replayed his hoarse cries in her mind, her own pleasured gasps as she'd attained peak after peak of bliss.

Bastien had helped her to explore the hitherto terrifying sensuality that had made her fear intimacy. And for that she'd always be grateful.

But the night was over.

Sitting up, she raked a slow hand through her tangled hair and tried to stem the deep yearning in her heart. She had no business yearning. She just had to focus on getting through the next few weeks. Then she could focus on the rest of her life.

Standing, she snatched up her clothes, deliberately keeping her gaze from the rumpled bed. Donning her skirt and top, she quickly left Bastien's room.

But, standing under the spray of the shower, Ana couldn't stop her hands caressing her skin. The deep knowledge that something fundamental had changed in her was unshakeable.

Unwilling to dwell on her thoughts, she hurriedly dressed in a grey linen skirt and a pink cashmere top. Leaving her hair loose, she applied a light gloss to her lips. Slipping her phone into her pocket, she went downstairs, her heart clambering into her throat at the thought of seeing Bastien again.

She found him at the dining table, showered and dressed in a blue shirt over which he wore a black sweater. She couldn't see the rest of his attire from where she lingered in the doorway, but she knew it would be no less immaculate. His head was bent over his newspaper, a lock of dark golden hair falling over his brow.

The yearning rushed back, fiercer than ever. Ana stood frozen in the doorway as the realisation of how much yearning she seemed to do around Bastien hit home.

He raised his head and speared her with those mesmerising eyes. With a casual flick of his wrist he discarded the paper, rose and approached her.

One hand traced her jaw, caressed it slowly until he captured her nape. Holding her still, he kissed her, deep and long.

Every single thought fled her head.

'Bonjour,' he greeted her when he lifted his head. 'You slept well.' It wasn't a question.

'Yes.'

He smiled. 'You must be hungry.' He led her to the table, waited until she'd sat, then offered fruit and poured her a cup of coffee. Slicing open a croissant, he buttered it, added a light spreading of jam—just the way she liked it—and passed it to her.

'Thank you,' Ana murmured, and took a bite, confusion warring with the flames of desire in her belly. She'd expected Bastien to return to his impassive best now that their night of passion was over. Instead he was being charming, pleasant.

'The production crew arrive tomorrow,' he said, biting into a halved peach. 'So today's your last day of leisure. What would you like to do?'

She blinked. 'Uh, if you don't mind I'd like to take Rebelle out for a ride.'

'That's one idea.'

His gaze drifted over her, triggering a blush that flooded her whole body. Her hands shook as she lowered her cup to its saucer.

'What's another?'

He casually reached out and traced her cheek with gentle fingers. 'I can ask Chantal to prepare a picnic lunch. We could take the boat on the lake this afternoon.'

Surprise followed by pleasure lit through her. 'Okay, you win. That sounds wonderful.'

His smile widened, causing her heart to hammer wildly. *'Bien.'* He motioned for her to eat and picked up his paper. 'I have a few things to attend to this morning. Meet me down at the pier at one.'

'Okay.' She half cringed at the breathy anticipation in her voice.

He quirked an eyebrow at her. 'What are your plans for the rest of the morning?'

'I noticed you have some audio books in your library. You don't mind me borrowing one, do you?' she asked.

A light frown touched his brows. 'Of course not.'

'Thanks.' Ana finished her meal and pushed back her chair.

'Wait.' He stood and walked her to the door.

Her heart dropped. Had she unwittingly given her secret away with her request? 'Yes…?'

Leaning forward, he dropped another kiss on her lips. 'Don't forget to dress warmly. The weather might be milder than expected but it can change, especially further north.'

Relief made her smile. 'Thanks.'

Ana escaped, her confusion rising to colossal proportions. Evidently morning-after etiquette didn't include a post-mortem of the night before. But did it include long, passionate kisses that reminded her of everything they'd done in bed together?

She wanted to ask him what he was playing at, but part of her was afraid that he'd stop. And the way she was going she wasn't above begging for a repeat performance.

The vibration of her phone as she entered the library brought welcome relief from her thoughts. Sliding it out of her pocket, she answered.

'Oh, *finally*. I've been trying to reach you since last night,' Lauren said.

Knowing why she'd been unreachable, Ana's face flamed. 'Sorry, my phone was set on vibrate,' she mumbled.

'I just wanted a quick catch-up. You normally call to discuss every clause in your contract, but this time you didn't. I was wondering why…'

She launched into her signature staccato burst of speech, forcing Ana to concentrate.

At first Ana couldn't believe what she was hearing. Dazed, she gripped the phone tighter, her heart sliding with dread into her stomach. 'Sorry, Lauren, can you repeat that, please?'

Lauren sighed and launched into another rapid-fire delivery.

By the time Ana ended the phone call she felt as if every single drop of blood had drained from her veins. She clutched the back of an armchair, struggling to breathe as Lauren's words rang through her brain.

Vaguely she heard the door open and close. Heard footsteps draw closer and Bastien's harsh curse.

'Ana! What's wrong?'

He sounded…*concerned*. But she knew she couldn't be hearing right. Knew it was a lie. How skilfully he'd fooled her!

From feeling faint, now she felt almost supernatural strength surge into her veins. She whirled and faced him.

'You bastard! You vile, despicable bastard.'

CHAPTER NINE

BASTIEN'S FACE HARDENED. 'I'm sure I can prove you wrong on the bastard issue, just as I'm sure you're about to enlighten me on these "vile, despicable" things I'm supposed to have done.'

'You know exactly what you've done. *More or less*—those were your words! God, how could I have been so stupid!'

Ana couldn't control her shaking or stem the deep well of pain springing up in her heart. She'd trusted him. She'd dropped her guard and given herself to him.

One brow lifted. 'I'm afraid you're not making any sense. Try again.'

'My contract!' Why couldn't she hold her voice steady? Why did it have to break now, when she needed to be strong? 'I trusted you.' She'd felt safe with him, foolishly let herself believe he wouldn't hurt her.

He exhaled slowly, a wash of bleakness blanking his features before he blinked it away. 'What about your contract?'

'You said it was "more or less" the same as the other one. Except you lied. It's so much more! Sleeping with me—was that a reward to yourself for successfully tricking me?'

His eyes grew arctic-cold. Stalking to where she stood, he grabbed her arm. 'You debase yourself with that assumption, Ana, and you debase me,' he breathed in soft, dangerous tones. 'I've never slept with anyone to secure a business deal.'

'A way of congratulating yourself for a job well done, then?'

He let go abruptly, as if he couldn't stand to touch her. 'I'm assuming this is how you feel about your contract. But I'm still in the dark as to how you think I've tricked you,' he incised.

'You *know* what you've done. My last contract was supposed to finish next month. Instead you've tied me into a contract for another year!'

'And I'm guessing you have a problem with that?'

'*No.* I'm flinging insults at you just for the hell of it. Deep down inside, Bastien, I'm actually dancing a jig.'

'Facetiousness doesn't suit you.'

'No? Perhaps you'd prefer me to come over there and claw your eyes out?'

Her voice broke again. And, damn it, tears welled in her eyes. They grew faster than she could stop them and spilled over before she could blink them away.

She swiped her cheeks with an angry hand. 'How *could* you, Bastien?'

'It's just business,' he replied coolly, but something flitted through his eyes, a slight softening as he traced her tearstained cheek.

'My *life* isn't just business. My *future* isn't just business!'

His brows clamped together. '*Je ne comprends pas.* You read the contract. Why did you sign it if you didn't agree with the terms?'

Her tears spilled faster, her shame closing in on her in a thick cloud of despair. She tried to look away, but Bastien's gaze had locked on hers with unwavering intensity. Her throat clogged with even more tears, her heart sinking as he came closer and grasped her shoulders.

'Why did you sign the contract, Ana?' he demanded.

She tried desperately to wrench herself out of his hold but he easily restrained her. More tears slid down her cheeks. She swallowed another sob, knowing there was no place to hide. 'Because I…I didn't want to admit that I…that I can't…'

His grip tightened. 'That you can't what?'

'That I can't *read*!'

His eyes widened. His jaw dropped along with his hands.

At any moment Ana knew his astonishment would be replaced with disgust. And she couldn't bear that—couldn't stand to see his revulsion at the realisation that he'd slept with someone who couldn't string two words together on a page.

Brushing past him, she fled the room. That he didn't stop her or even call out to her spoke volumes.

Ana didn't stop until she was outside, gasping in lungfuls of air as if they would stem the tears rolling freely down her face. But sobs continued to surge through her chest, released in agonising sounds that ripped through the morning air. She stumbled into the garden. Bypassing the koi pond, she ran until she found a bench on the far side of the grounds. Sinking down onto it, she dropped her face into her hands.

The secret she'd carried with her for more than half her life was out. Part of her felt relief that she no longer had to carry the heavy burden. But a larger part of her would have given anything to take it back. Because Bastien would never look at her the same way again. A man in his position wouldn't want to associate himself with anyone with her handicap. Who would want an illiterate model representing his world-class diamonds?

Fresh sobs clogged her throat. Defiantly, she swallowed them down. He'd lulled her into a false sense of security by letting her believe everything was above-board. It didn't sit well to acknowledge that part of it was her fault. She'd been so inclined to believe the good in Bastien that she'd dropped her vigilance when it came to her career.

She heard his approach a second before he emerged from behind a rose bush. Tall and powerful, he blocked out the bright sunshine when he stopped in front of her.

She turned away, hoping the curtain of her hair would hide her blotched, tearstained face.

'Go away, Bastien.' After all that had happened, after trusting him with her body, she just couldn't face him.

He didn't respond. Instead a square, neatly folded handkerchief appeared before her eyes. Mutely, she stared at it, wondered why it made her want to cry all over again.

She snatched it from him with curt thanks, tried to repair as much of the damage as possible and cringed when a hiccup escaped.

He folded his large frame on to the bench next to her and awareness of a different sort scythed through her as his thigh brushed hers. Surreptitiously she eased away.

If he noticed he didn't comment. Neither did he break the silence. It screeched on her nerves until, unable to stand it, she glanced furtively at him.

He was studying his hands, folded between his thighs. Sensing her gaze, his eyes locked with hers.

'The newspaper and the audio books?' he asked simply.

Face flaming, she nodded.

'Tell me,' he coaxed gently.

Her lips quivered and she looked away. 'I'd rather not.'

'It's nothing to be ashamed of, *ma petite*.' His voice was a low rumble. 'Dyslexia is a common—'

'I don't suffer from dyslexia. I can barely read or write because until I took matters into my own hands a year ago I'd never been taught how.' She waited for his revulsion, fresh tears stinging her eyes.

It never came. His eyes remained steady on hers, curiosity the only emotion she glimpsed in the silver depths.

'Why not?'

She heaved in a breath. 'At the time of my parents' divorce Lily was still modelling. When my father lost the custody battle he was devastated. He returned to Colombia and she immediately pulled me out of school with the excuse that she was taking me travelling and would hire tutors for me. And she did in the beginning. But she wouldn't pay the tutors and they would leave after a couple of months.

'I...I let something slip once to my father. She burned all my toys and called me an ungrateful child. After that she didn't bother to hide it from my father. She knew it would deeply upset him. He's a professor and education is his life. He reported her to the authorities a few times. She responded by banning me from seeing him for two years. When she signed me up with a modelling agency she warned me that if I let on about my lack of education I'd never see my father again. I was too scared to risk it so I…I lied to the agency when they asked if I was being tutored. Once I asked her why. She told me I was pretty enough. I didn't need an education.'

Bastien cursed under his breath. 'You mentioned a year ago. What changed?'

She took a deep breath. 'That's when I decided to stop modelling. My father was discussing his latest find with me. It was fascinating, and I told him I'd love to volunteer on one of his projects. But even as a volunteer I'd need basic qualifications. I found myself a tutor, and I've been making steady progress, but I get…overwhelmed under pressure.'

He gave a slight shake of his head, his eyes fixed on hers. 'And my asking you to sign a time-sensitive contract yesterday…' He cursed under his breath.

'I suppose you're disgusted?'

'*Mon Dieu*, of course I'm not disgusted,' he said, and the admission was faintly tinged with something else—something that sounded a lot like…admiration.

Ana inwardly shook her head. She was imagining things.

Abruptly, Bastien looked away. His gaze tracked two butterflies chasing each other from flower to flower. Then he reached into his pocket and extracted a sheaf of papers.

Ana's heart lurched as his large hands unfolded the document. She recognised her contract immediately.

'This agreement is made between Diamonds by Heidecker Incorporated, a subsidiary of the Heidecker Corporation, and Miss Ana Duval of—'

'Bastien, what are you doing?'

'I'm doing what I would've done if you'd told me. I'd never violate your trust, *ma petite*. If you don't believe anything else, believe that.'

He carried on reading, his deep, beautiful voice low and

hypnotic. Blinking back tears, she listened, her heart trembling as realisation sank in.

Bastien wasn't disgusted. He wasn't scornful that she couldn't read.

He was helping her.

Feelings, deep and inexplicable, flooded through her.

He read on, pausing every now and then to make sure she was paying attention. When he'd finished he glanced at her. 'You understood all that?'

Biting her lip to keep back the tears that seemed determined to ruin her, she nodded. 'Yes. You extended it by another year because you're thinking of serialising the ad campaign.'

'Yes. Would you have signed this contract if you'd known what you know now?'

She hesitated for a split second. 'No. I want to go and work with my father.'

He nodded. Then, without taking his eyes from hers, he tore the contract in two. Her gasp settled on the air before disintegrating against the sound of continued ripping. He shredded the paper until the sheets were tiny, insubstantial squares. Rolling them into a ball, he stuffed it in his pocket.

'Why?' she asked around a throat clogged with choking emotion.

His gaze turned sombre. 'You had no idea what you were signing. I won't take advantage of that.'

Simple words. Such simple words. Yet Ana felt the ground shift beneath her. Felt something cataclysmic rush through her, bringing back that sense of foreboding she'd felt as they drove through the gates of the chateau five days ago. But this time she caught a glimpse of what it meant before the moment was lost again. And she wasn't as frightened. What she *did* feel was an overwhelming need to touch Bastien, to connect with him—somehow convey this inexplicable feeling she couldn't give voice to.

Before she could stop herself she placed her hand on his cheek. 'If this carries on I'll start to think you're not as hard as you make yourself out to be.' Her voice emerged deeply husky, a result of her tears and the feelings roiling through her.

A small smile lifted one corner of his mouth. 'Don't fool yourself. I'm still the same.'

Her soft laugh wrapped around them. 'Maybe, but you're not so scary any more.'

He sobered. 'I scared you?'

'For a little while—and only because I didn't really know you well enough.'

'And you think you know me now?' A hint of wariness laced his tone, but he didn't move away.

'I'd like to…if you'd let me.' Knowing she was straying into forbidden territory made her shiver. But she forced herself to hold Bastien's gaze even when it hardened slightly.

'There's nothing to know. I told you: I'm a simple man.'

With deep undercurrents of emotional baggage. Ana let it go, but she couldn't stop herself from leaning forward to kiss him lightly on the lips. He immediately deepened the kiss, stamping his mastery on the act until they both had to come up for air.

'Thank you,' she muttered when she could speak.

'What for?' he breathed against her lips.

'For listening and for not being repulsed by my inability to read.'

He twisted his head, kissed her palm and folded her hand in his. 'Being unable to read or write doesn't define who you are. Don't be ashamed of it.' Standing up, he reached for her. 'We'll discuss your new contract later. I need to make a few calls before we head out for the picnic.'

'We're still going?' she asked, surprised.

'Nothing has changed, Ana.'

Her heart lifted, but almost immediately sank again. He might have just shown her that the kind, considerate fifteen-year-old she'd caught a glimpse of still existed somewhere in the adult Bastien. But that was as far as their situation went.

Their one-night agreement still stood. She was still his employee. And he was still giving out 'Do Not Trespass' signals.

And yet Ana knew *she* had changed. And with that change had come a deep yearning to fight for what she wanted.

And she wanted Bastien.

The truth of the statement hit her like a bolt of lightning.

As she walked beside him through the garden back to the château she couldn't help glancing at him. He wasn't as closed-off as he'd been a few days ago. The tightness around his mouth and eyes had eased, and the impassive look she'd associated with him at the beginning had dissipated. But she'd seen another side of him now. Perhaps, with time, he might even let her in.

Bastien caught her glance. 'What's wrong?'

She shook her head. 'Nothing. I'll go and freshen up and meet you here in an hour.'

Bastien finished his calls in half that time but deliberately stayed in his study, even though he wanted to shove back his chair and hunt her down. The confusion that had assailed him in the middle of the night when he'd watched her sleep had returned, intensified, since her stark announcement that morning.

He didn't know what to do with the rush of protectiveness he'd felt when he'd seen her pain. Nor his undeniable need to seek her out in the garden, make sure she was all right.

Destroying the contract had been a no-brainer once he knew.

His jaw tightened. Lily Duval had wronged her daughter on so many levels. His own parents' callous rejection had eroded any thoughts of a family of his own from his mind well before he'd emerged from teenhood. A life of solitude with the occasional liaison suited him fine. But Ana, despite her mother's treatment of her, had forgiven her over and over. Bastien found it hard to grasp that forgiving spirit. But he couldn't deny that he found it humbling…that it forced him to examine his relationship with his parents.

He glanced at the phone, found himself reaching for it. This time he dialled the number even as his senses reeled. He listened to the echoing ring, then the answer machine clicked in.

He cleared his throat. 'Maman, *c'est moi*, Bastien… I…I'll

call back tomorrow.' He dropped the phone and speared a hand through his hair.

What the hell was happening to him? What the hell was he doing, risking rejection all over again?

His every thought seemed to go back to Ana. She was responsible for this madness. For this upheaval in his life. The wisest thing would be to stay away from her.

He surged to his feet, but his intended path to the window veered off course when he heard her voice outside his study. Her fist was poised to knock. Her eyes, devoid of the tears that had slashed at his insides earlier, clashed with his.

'Our picnic's ready. Do you want me to take it down to the pier?'

Glancing down, he saw the large basket at her feet, but almost immediately his attention was riveted on her legs displayed beneath the skirt of her sundress.

A tremor coursed through him, displacing thought and reason and creating a vivid picture of how those legs had felt wrapped around him.

With more force than necessary he grasped the handle of the basket and yanked it up. 'It's all right. I'm ready to leave.'

She fell into step beside him. Bastien tried not to inhale her scent greedily.

They walked down to the pier and he saw her surprise when they reached his twenty-foot navy blue cabin cruiser.

'I thought the boat would be a replica of your big, flashy super-yacht moored in Cannes. Or is that only for seducing the employees you want to fire?'

He slid her a glance. 'What happened on that boat has only happened once. With you.'

He helped her in and passed her the basket. Their fingers touched and she trembled. Resisting the urge to cancel the trip and sweep her off into his bed, he started the engine and eased away from the pier.

'Where are we going?' she asked.

'We're headed upstream to Villeneuve.'

They picked up speed and Ana threw back her head, a wide smile on her face as she enjoyed the rush of the breeze.

Bastien watched her wave to other sailors, unable to take his eyes off her. When she glanced at him the look in her eyes stopped his breath. Forcing himself to concentrate or risk crashing, he pulled the boat into a tiny inlet and pointed to a hill above them.

'There's a spot just over that rise. We'll have lunch there.'

They reached the top of the hill and she gazed down at the view. 'It's beautiful,' she said.

'Indeed,' he agreed.

She turned and Bastien's gaze dropped to her mouth. Relentless desire pounded at him. She swayed as if the force of his need had physically reached out and tugged her to him.

Last night had done nothing to ease his hunger, he admitted grimly to himself. If anything, it had only intensified his yearning for her.

That didn't mean he had to act on it. Turning away, he briskly laid out their lunch, gesturing to her to take her place opposite him.

Tucking her hair behind her ears, Ana sank onto the blanket. 'Is there anything I can do to help?'

'Grab a plate and dish out the food. The bread should still be warm. I'll cut up some cheese after I pour the wine,' he said.

He filled a crystal glass and passed it to her. Her slim fingers brushed his. He heard her faint gasp and forced himself to ignore it.

'The weather is much cooler than I imagined it would be at this time of year.'

'To Genevans this is positively arctic weather.'

'You're very lucky. I hate being cold.'

'Then why do you live in London?'

She shrugged. 'That's where I grew up. But I won't be for much longer.'

'Archaeology is a huge change.'

She took a bite of her food and chewed before answering. 'I love a challenge.'

His wry smile confirmed that observation. 'Most women would give everything to be in your place. And the paparazzi certainly loves you.' He watched her, twirling his wine glass lazily between his fingers.

'I'm not most women. And I don't court publicity, if that's what you're implying. What I do is part of my job—'

'It's part of your job to constantly appear in public wearing as little as possible, hanging off the arm of the latest male model?' A dark emotion stormed through his gut and his fingers tightened around his glass.

'You'd be surprised how often the same pictures are modified and reused. Anyway, how do you know? Have you been checking up on me?'

Bastien felt a dull flush creep across his cheeks. He refused to admit he'd taken more than a little interest in her since she'd become the model for the DBH campaign.

When her eyes collided with his, heat flared within him. 'I take a healthy interest for professional reasons.'

She laughed. 'Really? Are you saying a powerful businessman like you doesn't have minions to check things like that for you?' Her voice had grown husky and her head had tilted seductively.

He grew hotter. He took a few bites of food as emotions tumbled through him.

They'd long passed civilised conversation and moved on to the subtext of sex and feelings that seemed inevitably to spring up between them when they were alone. His gaze flicked down to her mouth, her throat, caressed her neck and settled on her chest before climbing back up.

Her tongue snuck out, moistened her plump lips, and right then he would have given anything in the world to taste those lips again.

But he had to end this fevered need that clawed at him every time he looked at her. 'Don't look at me like that, *ma petite*.'

'Like what?' she challenged. 'Help me out here, Bastien. I don't know how this works. You kiss me when you feel like it, touch me, hold my hand. But I can't *look* at you?'

His jaw tightened. 'You don't just look. You beguile with every sigh, tempt me with every breath.'

Hurt fleeted through her eyes, making him feel deeply unsettled.

'I'm not deliberately trying to.'

He half laughed, half groaned. 'I know. That's the problem.'

'Has it even occurred to you that I react like that because I'm attracted to you?'

Bastien was used to women speaking plainly about what they wanted from him—sometimes explicitly. Ana wasn't one of them. He'd witnessed her struggle before succumbing to the incredible chemistry between them last night. The same way she'd struggled with revealing her painful relationship with her mother.

But the last thing he wanted, or needed, was for her to confuse their sexual encounter with something else. Or, worse, read some deeper meaning into the act. Emotion was messy. Emotion led to heartbreak and rejection.

She cleared her throat. 'Last night—'

He cut in. 'Last night was all it can ever be.'

Boldly, she met his gaze. 'Why?'

'Because letting temptation and emotion rule my life would make me no better than—' He stopped, shock stabbing him at what he'd almost revealed.

'Than who? Your father? That was what you were going to say, wasn't it?'

He jerked upright and walked to the crest of the hill, staring down at the lake.

'Leave it, Ana.' He growled the warning.

'But I guessed right, didn't I? What are you so afraid of?'

He whirled. 'Afraid! You think I'm *afraid*?'

'Well…what, then? You won't let yourself feel, and you snarl at anyone who attempts to get to know you.'

His laugh sounded edgy even to his own ears. 'You'd prefer me to wear my heart on my sleeve like some paperback hero?'

'No, but you told me this morning not to be ashamed of my shortcomings. You're letting the sins of your parent shape the way you live your life.'

'Parents. Plural.' His eyes met hers. 'What about you? Did you not hang on to your virginity because you didn't want to end up like your mother?'

'Yes, but I'm not a virgin any more,' she pointed out softly. 'And I'm trying very hard not to be like my mother.'

The deep conviction in her voice sparked something inside him. Something he realised, to his chagrin, was jealousy. Somewhere between his rescuing her from the courtroom and now she had attained a certain unshakeable confidence that had nothing to do with her poise or profession.

He stared at her, compelled, unable to take his eyes off her as she took another step closer.

'What happened sixteen years ago was terrible. I was there too, remember? But at least your parents found their way back together and stayed together. You were lucky.'

Harsh laughter erupted from a place of dark, shuddering pain he thought he'd sealed off for ever.

'Lucky! You call living with a serial adulterer of a father who didn't bother to hide his transgressions from his family and a mother who instead of protecting her son tried to take her own life in the most dramatic way possible, *lucky*?'

CHAPTER TEN

ANA STRUGGLED TO BREATHE. 'What?'

'You heard me,' he rasped, his voice raw and pain-filled.

'But I thought… Oh, Bastien, I'm so sorry.' Her chest felt tight, but it had nothing to do with her asthma. All she felt was overwhelming compassion for what Bastien had suffered.

'Forget it.' He dismissed her words with a shrug.

She tried to take a breath but only a distressed wheeze emerged.

Bastien's gaze sharpened. 'What's wrong?' he demanded.

She tried to shake her head but he was already taking her arm. One finger urged her face up to his, where concern was etched.

'Nothing. I'm fine. When did your mother try to take her own life?'

He dropped his hand. 'Not now. We need to get back.'

'Bastien, please talk to me—'

'Unless you want to get caught in the rain we need to get moving.'

She glanced up at the sky, surprised to notice storm clouds rolling over the lake. Whilst they'd been locked in the past the weather had changed.

She helped him pack their picnic away, despite his terse instruction to let him do it. They returned to the boat in silence, even though she felt his concerned glance more than once.

Placing the basket in the tiny galley, he led her to the single cabin. 'Stay down here. If the rain hits the journey back might be a little bumpy.'

'I'll stay here if you'll promise me we'll talk when we get back.'

He blew out an exasperated breath. '*Oui*, we'll talk,' he said. And left.

Ana tried to relax, but her thoughts churned. Bastien's parents had stayed together but the circumstances she'd imagined, the assumptions she'd made, were very far from the truth. Another wave of empathy surged through her.

She headed for the door, but paused and groaned when she caught her image in the mirror beside the bed.

Her skin was pale, her eyes wide pools of anguish. And some time between leaving the château and now her hair had become a tangled web. She thought of repairing the mess, but gave up.

The outward mess she could deal with later. It was the inner mess that terrified her—because she feared the path her heart had taken was fraught with danger.

Bastien steered the boat alongside the pier, his thoughts grim. What the hell had happened on that hill in Villeneuve? How had he let go of his control so much that he'd spilled the cause of his deepest pain to Ana?

Revealing what his mother's ultimate rejection had done to him was inexcusable. He'd thought that particular fear was buried deep, unreachable.

But all it had taken was one softly voiced challenge to send him back to that dark, harrowing place.

Jumping onto the pier, he secured the rope with a vicious twist, silently thankful that the production crew were arriving tomorrow. The earlier he wrapped the ad campaign, the earlier he could end this enforced hiatus and return to his life. A life devoid of Ana, devoid of heated looks from sultry chocolate-brown eyes. No more second-guessing the choices he'd made for a life without emotion. A life that stretched out bleak and empty at the thought of Ana not being a part of it...

With a muted curse, he turned. She stood at the top of the steps leading to the galley, one hand lifted to catch her hair as the breeze played with it.

Bastien's breath strangled in his chest. Just looking at her made his world fracture, threatening to splinter into a million pieces. No matter how much he tried to wrestle back control everything in him wanted to stride over to her, snatch her tiny waist in his hands and devour her lips. Maybe then they'd both forget what he'd let slip on the hillside.

As if she'd read his thoughts she parted her lips. Desire arrowed straight to his groin, leaving him as weak as a day-old kitten. That in itself was such a shock he couldn't move for several seconds.

In all his affairs no woman had ever brought such an intense, debilitating feeling to him. Such…*freedom*. As if he was poised on the brink of some cataclysmic discovery.

Pour l'amour de Dieu. He stepped back into the boat and retrieved the basket. All this idle time was addling his brain. Facts. Figures. Cut-throat negotiations. That was what he needed. Not Ana back in his bed. That was *not* going to happen.

They entered the château through the kitchen, where Chantal was putting groceries away in the large pantry. He thanked her for the picnic and left the basket on the counter.

As he turned to leave, he caught sight of a tiny picture by the window. Stunned, he moved towards it, even though the image was one he remembered very well.

It was his father, his mother and himself on the pier, taken when he was five or six. They all looked so…*happy*. He picked up the picture, rubbing his hand across the dusty surface.

'I kept it from…before,' Chantal said from just behind his shoulder. 'I hope you don't mind.'

Before… When he'd moved back here and ordered everything that reminded him of his parents to be boxed up and shipped to Gstaad.

Without warning, Ana's words echoed in his mind. *'You're letting the sins of your parent shape the way you live your life.'*

He set the picture down, fighting endless waves of disquiet. But this time the righteous anger that usually fuelled his bitterness was missing. Was she right? Had he let what had happened sixteen years ago dictate the way he lived?

He turned. Ana stood in the doorway, her eyes seeking, her skin pale.

That jolt came again—harder than before. The chocolate depths were clear, fringed by lashes so thick and luxurious most women would kill to own them.

As if she couldn't stand his blatant scrutiny she dropped her lids. That didn't stop the arresting power of her face. His gaze moved down to the sensual curve of her lips and his chest tightened. How many times during the night had he tasted their sweetness? Yet he craved another taste so badly he could barely breathe.

He watched as colour rose in her cheeks. Knowing she wasn't over this crazy chemistry between them either did nothing to ease his suffering.

Get a grip.

'I need to clean up,' she said.

Relief poured through him. 'Okay. We'll talk later.'

When he'd had a chance to regroup.

He went straight to his study and poured himself a brandy. Taking it to the terrace, he watched the sun set on his favourite lake. Nothing in the scene soothed him the way it normally did.

Prowling to the edge of the terrace, he lifted his face to the cool breeze washing in from the water.

His work was his life. Had been for as long as he could remember. Yet what he yearned for now, above everything else, was to be upstairs with Ana, losing himself in her body. Even the 'we need to talk' that normally sent him running didn't eradicate this intense need to be with her.

He was definitely losing it!

Knocking back the rest of the drink, he returned to his study.

He entered the words into the search engine of his laptop and read through the information that came up. Satisfied he'd found what he needed, he closed the programme, then paused mid-stretch as he heard Ana's voice in the hallway.

He'd lunged towards the door before he'd fully recognised his intentions.

She'd changed into a dark orange shift dress that set off her golden skin so spectacularly he had to shove his hands into his pockets to stop them from reaching for her. Her loose dark hair rippled with vitality, caressed one cheek as she turned. Slim fingers tucked the strands behind her ears, a small smile appearing on her lips when she saw him.

'Are you hungry?'

She grimaced. 'Not really. My appetite seems to have taken a hike.'

She started walking towards the library. He fell into step beside her, opened the door and let her precede him, trying not to get too lost in her subtle perfume. Feeling like a geeky teenager caught gawping at the hottest girl in class, he plucked the nearest book from the shelf and cleared his throat.

'I have something for you. Come.'

She glanced at him, but said nothing as she followed him to his study. A smaller laptop sat next to his large one. He turned it towards her.

'Sit down,' he said.

Too surprised to protest, she sat. He pressed a button on the small laptop and the screen flickered to life. 'I'm not sure what your tutor was using before, but I've found a programme to tutor you in basic reading and writing. Do you use a laptop at home?' he asked.

Flushing slightly, she nodded. 'Yes.'

'Good.' He guided her through the simple programme until she could manage on her own. Then he handed her the laptop. 'This one's yours. We'll have a lesson every morning after breakfast. Make no mistake: I will be hard on you if I think you're slacking— Why are you biting your lip?'

'Because I'm trying to stop myself from crying, you idiot.'

That protective instinct he'd been trying to stave off washed over him when her eyes filled. He found himself crouching before her, cupping her cheek before he could stop himself. Hell, there was no denying it. Ana undid him like no other person on earth.

'If you're trying to find a way to make me go softer on you, forget it.'

She laughed and the sound suffused his veins with happiness. When she bent her head and a swathe of hair covered part of her face he tucked it behind her ear.

'Why are you doing this, Bastien?'

He stilled, searched for a flippant answer but failed. 'Because you're a generous, talented person and you deserve someone in your corner.'

Her beautiful eyes filled again and he cursed under his breath.

'But on the hill you said—'

'I shouldn't have ripped into you like that.' His smile felt strained. 'Truth is, no one has ever dared to examine my baggage so closely. No one has ever been allowed close enough to try. Except you. Hell, I even called my mother today because of your pushing. I'm thinking of heading to Gstaad when the shoot is over. Will you come with me?'

Her eyes lit up. 'If you want me to.' She reached out and touched his knee. 'Tell me what happened with her. Please—I want to know,' she implored softly.

Bastien swallowed. That he was even considering sharing any more of his painful past with her surprised the hell out of him.

'Are you sure? It gets a little messy,' he warned, aware that his voice was huskier than usual.

She pursed her lips and waited.

He leaned forward and rested his elbows on his knees. 'Do you remember that last day at Verbier? You may have been too young—'

'I remember.' Her smile was poignant. 'Your mother turned up out of the blue and demanded to see your father. Lily was screaming vile things at your father...'

He clenched his jaw. 'And he was busy taking out his anger on my mother. They spoke in French, so you didn't understand, of course. He told her she had no right to be there. That he was done with her pathetic, needy clinging.'

Ana flinched. He smoothed his thumbs down her cheeks.

'He said was leaving her—divorcing her as soon as they returned to Geneva.'

'Oh, Bastien...'

He shook his head, a cold, icy hand clamping over his chest where for a long time he'd remained frozen. 'Here's the kicker. He told her if she intended to fight for me he wouldn't stand in her way. And she...' An old wound, never really healed, split open, throwing him back sixteen years, so that his parents' voices were as clear as if they were in the room with him now, 'She said if she couldn't have my father then she didn't want me.'

Ana gasped and threw her arms around him. He held her tight, reeling from the remembered rejection even as he acknowledged that the pain he'd felt all these years was considerably less this time around. As if baring his soul to Ana had washed away the rough edges of anguish.

'Oh, my God, Bastien. I'm so sorry. I had no idea,' she murmured softly.

He finally pulled back, focused on her crouched before him. One hand touched his cheek and he exhaled noisily. She was offering comfort. When had that *ever* happened to him? He'd forged his way through life on his own after that stark double rejection sixteen years ago. And he'd succeeded. Hell, he more than succeeded. He'd excelled at everything he'd ever set his mind to.

He glanced into Ana's face, ready to tell her to save her pity for someone else. Tears shone in her eyes.

'You're crying again.'

'No child should hear that from anyone—most of all their parent.'

'You cry for *me* even after all you've suffered?'

His voice sounded strange in his own ears, and that tight band around his chest loosened. Shaken by the feelings rolling over him, he caught a tear from her cheek with his thumb.

'Maybe I cry for both of us.' Slowly she raised herself up on her knees and kissed his cheek—one, then the other. 'I'm sorry for both of us.'

Bastien wanted to catch her to him, to hold her tight and never let her go. And that thought above everything else unsettled him, shook him to his core, made him pull away from her.

'Don't be. It was a lesson well learnt. People use love as a tool to hurt each other. My mother tried to take her own life because she loved my father too much to watch him with another woman. She never once stopped to think of her son or how her actions would affect *him*.'

She rocked back. 'You think she betrayed you?'

'No, I don't. In fact I don't think she was thinking about me at all. She was thinking only of herself—obsessed with living in fairytales, searching for that elusive happy-ever-after.'

Clenching her hands in her lap, she swallowed. 'Love isn't a fairytale.'

'No, it's an excuse people use to hurt to each other. Every time I think I can forgive her I remember that she chose the most dramatic way possible to demonstrate her so-called love. A love that didn't include me.'

Ana swallowed, trying to dislodge the lump of pain that had taken root there since Bastien had started speaking. Her heart ached for him. The thought of the toll his mother's action had taken on him tore at her insides.

'Did you…were you the one who found her?'

He frowned down at her. 'No. Don't you remember?'

Puzzled, Ana shook her head. 'I'm sorry. I don't think so…'

'You don't the remember the chaos after my father and Lily returned a few hours later?'

'Yes, I do, but—' Shock stopped her breath. 'Are you saying *that's* when your mother tried to…?'

Bitterness twisted his lips. 'And she almost succeeded. The doctors said another half an hour and she'd have been dead.'

'But *how*?'

Ana remembered the sad, broken figure of Solange Heidecker. Ana had been in one of the guest rooms, hiding after the screams had lapsed into an eerie silence, when the door had opened. Solange had walked in, looked around, and immediately turned to leave. At the last moment she'd seen Ana and slowly approached. Even at her young age the melancholy surrounding Bastien's mother had struck her.

'Which is your mother's room, *mon enfant*? Come and show me.' She'd held out her hand.

Ana had shown her, had stood in the doorway as she'd inspected every item of clothing, every shoe, every trinket in the room. Finally she'd sunk onto the bed, tears coursing down her face. Ana remembered her own sadness, remembered feeling in some way responsible for the woman's pain.

She'd watched Solange take her shoes off slowly and lie back on the bed. 'I'm not feeling very well, *cherie*.' She'd smiled another sad, heartbreaking smile. 'Please ask the housekeeper to bring me something for my headache, would you?'

Icy fingers of dread clamped around Ana's heart. Her vision clouded, a dizzying faintness overcoming her.

No! No, no—

'Ana!' Bastien's voice came from a far distance, from beyond the vacuum closing around her.

Oh, please God, no…

Her whole body had gone numb and her heart was beating dully, as if preparing to stop beating altogether. Bastien's hands gripped her shoulders, but even his firm shake couldn't force Ana from the dark fog of the past.

What had she done? Dear God, what had she done?

'Ana, talk to me. What is it?'

The urgency in his voice finally scraped the edges of her consciousness. Slowly his face swam into view. Her heart ached at its perfect beauty, at the hard, impassive edge he portrayed to the world, at the concern he couldn't help but feel—because deep down Bastien was just a man whose heart ached for love, just as hers did.

Most of all her heart was ripped open at the knowledge that *she* was the cause of his pain. That she had helped shape him into the hardened cynic he was today.

Tears blistered the back of her eyes. 'I'm so sorry, Bastien. Oh God, I…I'm so sorry.' Her voice broke and a sob dredged from the very depths of her pulverised soul erupted through her lips.

'For what?'

'Your mother. She took pills, didn't she?' The words scraped her throat, as if rebelling against being aired.

A frown slowly gathered on his brow. 'Yes, but how…?'

'She… Oh, God, Bastien… She didn't try to commit suicide. I think she overdosed by accident. And I…I gave her the pills.'

CHAPTER ELEVEN

BASTIEN'S FACE, NORMALLY a vibrant, masculine hue, paled. It was almost as if he'd turned to stone, so statue-still he became. His eyes reflected shock. Horrified, disbelieving shock.

'Non, il n'est pas possible!'

His lips barely moved with the denial, but his fingers tightened painfully on her shoulders.

'That is not possible, Ana. She came to Verbier with the express purpose of…' His words trailed off and he swallowed, his eyes darkening with remembered pain.

Ana's heart twisted. 'You weren't there, Bastien. You were in the gazebo. She asked me to get pills from the housekeeper for her headache. Lily always kept a bottle of pills on her bedside table. She…she told me they were for her headaches. Oh, God, I didn't…couldn't read the label. I…I gave them to your mother—'

'How many did she take?'

'I don't remember—'

He thrust her away from him, surged to his feet. He stalked to the window, his movements stiff, wooden. For several seconds he said nothing, then he whirled to face her. *'Mon Dieu!'* The hand he shoved through his hair shook badly.

'I'm sorry,' she whispered brokenly.

'And all this time I've believed—' He stopped, fists clenched at his sides.

A deep shudder raked through his frame and her heart twisted anew.

'I'm so sorry… Oh, God!'

He crossed the room and caught her arms. 'Stop apologising, Ana. You were eight years old and you couldn't read. You are *not* to blame for this!'

'But if I'd called someone instead of just handing her the pills…' She clamped her hand over her lips, racked with horror. 'The repercussions of that day have shaped your life, Bastien. What I did has coloured the way you see your mother for the last sixteen years…'

He shook her once, the act almost one of desperation. 'No, it hasn't. Don't forget the things she said before she took the pills. You had nothing to do with that. That was *her*…all her.' Renewed pain threaded his voice.

Ana wanted to offer something, anything to soothe his pain. Except *she* was the cause of his pain.

'Let me go, Bastien.'

'No, you wanted to talk, so we'll talk about this.'

'There's nothing left to talk about. I ruined your life—'

'No, dammit, *listen* to me.'

'There's nothing you can say that'll make me forgive myself, Bastien. Nothing.' She pulled away and ran to the door.

Thankfully, he didn't follow.

Her whole body trembled with the force of her emotions as she climbed the stairs to her room. She collapsed on the bed, her legs unwilling to support her as renewed shock ripped through her. She drew a pillow to her face to muffle the sound of the wrenching sobs that rumbled through her chest.

She had caused Solange Heidecker's overdose.

She had ripped Bastien's life apart!

Her tears fell faster, her insides quaking with the force of her pain. His father's affairs had made Bastien bitter, but Ana realised it was his mother's rejection and suicide attempt that had flayed him. Discovering he'd spent the last sixteen years hating his mother for something she hadn't meant to do had rocked him. Ana had seen his shock when he'd realised this.

How could Bastien ever forgive her?

She woke bleary-eyed and heavy-hearted the next morning to the sound of knocking on her door. Her heart lurched, but it was Chantal who greeted her when she wrenched open the door, not Bastien.

'*Bonjour, mademoiselle.* Your crew…they have arrived.'

'Oh…okay. Thanks,' she murmured, licking lips stiff with dried tears. She caught Chantal's quick scrutiny before she started to turn away. She'd fallen asleep in her clothes and still clutched a tissue she'd used some time during the night. 'Wait! Is Bastien…is he awake yet?' She didn't know how to begin to repair the damage she'd done but she'd lain awake knowing she had to start somewhere.

Chantal shook her head, her eyes solemn. '*Non. Monsieur*—he left last night.'

Misery and pain spiked through her, their bite so ferocious she folded her arms around her middle in self-preservation. 'Left? When will he be back?'

The housekeeper shrugged.

Dazed, Ana closed the door. Bastien had left, and taken with him any opportunity to ask for his forgiveness.

The thought of him suffering because of what she'd done brought fresh tears. But Ana brushed them away and sucked in a deep breath. He was gone. She couldn't do anything about that. What she *could* do, though, was throw her every last skill at making the ad campaign the best it could be. *That* she could control.

Trudging to the bathroom, she undressed and showered.

The crew's arrival threw the château into a whirlwind of frenzied activity. Ana gladly submerged herself in the organised chaos, helping to unload equipment and assisting Chantal in setting up the crew in their allocated rooms. Anything to stop herself from revisiting that desolate place inside her that threatened to overwhelm her every time she thought of Bastien.

The first fracture in her false façade came when her phone beeped with a text. Thinking it was from Bastien, she jumped on it—only to find it was from Lily, wishing her luck for the shoot. The hope she'd been trying to stem since that phone call with her mother refused to die, no matter how much she tried to stave it off.

Her composure slipped even further when, at midday, a lawyer from a local firm turned up. He'd been hired by Bastien the day before and instructed to help her redraft new terms for her contract.

The short, moustachioed man was visibly startled when tears welled in her eyes. Bastien had shortened the twelve-month contract to two, and given her first refusal for any serialised campaigns. She signed the documents, her heart aching.

'Ana—there you are.'

She turned from the late-afternoon sunlight streaming through the tower window to find Robin Green, the director, behind her.

'Okay, that forlorn look you were wearing just now is great for when we shoot the scene downstairs, moments before you meet your handsome prince again after seven years apart. But not for the tower scene. Remember—this room is where love finally triumphs. I want radiance, ecstasy, unforgettable passion. Yes?'

She nodded, although deep inside she despaired about how she could pull off everlasting love when her insides were anguished, raw.

All through hair and make-up her mind drifted, wondering where Bastien was, what he was doing. How he was coping with the bombshell she'd thrown into his life.

Her emotions were so on edge a lump rose in her throat when the two security men guarding the Heidecker diamonds stepped forward. The white diamonds selected for the first scene were dazzling. As always, Ana was awed at the beauty of the pieces the Heidecker jewellers had produced. She'd modelled countless pieces of jewellery before, but none as stunning as the award-winning Diamonds by Heidecker collection.

She held her breath as the necklace was fastened. Against the royal blue of her floor-length strapless Dior gown the stones of the diamond collarette set in platinum stood out so vividly even the seasoned make-up artist gave a murmur of appreciation. Matching teardrop earrings went on next.

Xander Bryson took the role of her childhood love, the prince, but the scene they were shooting now required her to play alongside her current lover, on whose arm she was to arrive at a ball.

Robin yelled, 'Action!'

A limousine rolled forward and the flashes of fake paparazzi cameras erupted as Ana stepped from the car onto the red carpet. Faking sadness came easily. Her actions had permanently scarred the beautiful man who owned her heart, so she immersed herself in her heartache and went with it.

'That was *perfection*, Ana,' Robin gushed. 'Always a great sign when things go so well on a first take. Keep it up and we'll have this thing wrapped in three days.'

Unfortunately the second day went in the opposite direction. Rain disrupted half a day's shoot, fraying tempers and causing diva fits from Xander.

By the middle of day three Ana's feet hurt and her whole body was mired in physical and emotional exhaustion. Striking poses for the photographer in charge of taking the stills—a tyrant who hid behind a perfectionist label—wasn't going as smoothly as the filming had.

She heard the photographer's annoyed huff one more time and suppressed her own huff. She wanted to scream, to tell him to take his camera and shove it somewhere dark and disturbing.

Swallowing her irritation, she tried another pose.

With another curse the photographer lowered his camera. 'This isn't working, Ana. Your shoulders are all hunched up. Relax!'

She gritted her teeth.

'Think of something evocative…naughty. A lover kissing the back of your neck.' He smirked.

Heat unfurled in her stomach as the image of Bastien doing exactly that rose in her mind. Her cheeks flushed, her body reacting instantly.

'Yes! That's it. Now, look straight into the camera!'

Ana responded to the directive automatically. The shutter clicked several times before she could wipe the look off her face. Shame drenched her as the photographer crooned his approval. Even after she'd lowered her eyes he clicked away.

The minute he took a break she sprang to her feet and rushed out, but the refrain in her head wouldn't stop.

She loved him.

She loved Bastien.

The knowledge swamped her, wrapped tight around her heart, sent a dizzying wave of warmth through her even as her heart broke with the knowledge that she'd never have him.

Keep it together. Keep it together.

Somehow she made it through the rest of the afternoon and the next day without crumbling into a heap of pathetic hopelessness and bawling her eyes out.

Perhaps Robin was right and she *was* a natural, because she even managed the passion required for the final tower scene in which her onscreen lover presented her with the Crown Jewel— the signature marquise-cut yellow Heidecker diamond.

By simply closing her eyes and imagining she was kissing Bastien the scene was shot in a single take.

And, best of all, no one knew her heart was breaking into a million little pieces.

CHAPTER TWELVE

THE SHOOT WRAPPED just after midday, only half a day later than scheduled. Ana's bags were packed, Bastien was gone and she had no right to be here when he returned. She had no intention of sullying the Château D'Or with her presence for longer than necessary.

She was packing away the last of the clothes Bastien had bought her when Xander entered her room and plonked himself on the antique armchair.

'You're coming out tonight, right?'

Tatiana had booked an exclusive restaurant and bar in Montreux for the wrap party but Ana had no interest in celebrating. 'I was thinking of giving it a miss—'

'No way. You're the belle of the ball. You don't go— I don't go.'

'Xander—'

'There won't be any paps around, if that's what you're worried about.'

She shook her head. 'It's not.'

His face became unusually thoughtful. 'Are you worried about those absurd drug charges?'

She froze. In the midst of falling in love with a man she could never have she'd shoved all thoughts of her upcoming trial to the back of her mind. They flooded back now. 'Absurd or not, they're real.'

He nodded. 'Do you have any idea who put the hook into you?'

'No, but thanks for not assuming I'm guilty.'

He rolled his eyes. 'Please—you go green if anyone so much as mentions taking an aspirin. You could be the poster child for a universal anti-drug campaign.'

'That doesn't give me any idea of who did it.'

He eyed her silently for several seconds, making her heart race.

'Xander…?'

'I'm not pointing fingers, but perhaps you need to look closer to home for the culprit. And I mean *home* in the literal sense.'

Her heart lurched. 'Are you sure?'

He shrugged. 'All I'm saying is explore that avenue thoroughly.' He jumped up and pecked her on the cheek. 'Now, doll yourself up. It's time to *par-tay.*'

About to refuse again, she paused.

She was in love with a man she'd wronged beyond forgiveness. In the middle of the night, racked with pain and guilt, she'd toyed with calling Tatiana to find out where he was. In the end she'd decided the best thing to do was to give him his space.

There would be time for nursing her broken heart later. Once she was far away from here.

She'd achieved what she'd set out to do for Bastien—salvage his ad campaign. To cause tongues to wag now would undo all the good she'd done, and refusing to attend the party would do just that.

'Okay, I'll come.'

Xander whooped on his way out, his fingers flying over the keyboard of his phone.

She chose a designer outfit that was more of a tunic than a dress. Its large sleeves covered her arms, but the bold, colourful, striped dress stopped at mid-thigh. Hoping it lent her an urgently needed vibrancy, she cinched it with a bronze diamante-studded belt and bronze high heels. Leaving her hair loose, she expertly applied her make-up and headed downstairs.

The trip to Montreux took less than half an hour.

The Hotel Suisse's Belle Epoque private dining suite had

been reserved exclusively for their use. Appreciative murmurs went through a crowd who, even used to working in an industry of blatant wealth, weren't used to such extravagance.

Ana tried to feel joy in her surroundings but failed miserably. Desolation crashed over her, closely followed by the pain she felt every time she thought of Bastien.

She loved him. He would never love her.

But, with time, would he love another? Jealousy, hot and fierce, seared her at the thought of him married, perhaps raising children with another woman. By the time that happened—please God—she'd be at the opposite end of the earth with no access to newspapers or television. Because Ana didn't think she could stand it. She couldn't stand thinking about it now—

'Hey, Ana, my Twitter fans are asking about you. You want to say something to them?' Xander shoved his phone under her nose.

She froze, the familiar wave of shame gripping her as she stared at the phone.

'Type in any message you want.'

She took the phone and carefully typed in five letters, feeling a quiet sense of triumph when she succeeded. Xander looked at the screen.

'"Hello"? That's all you're going to say to two million fans? Try something sexy and scandalous!'

'I seriously advise against that if you want to keep working for me, Mr Bryson.'

Ana's head snapped up at the sound of the deep voice. Bastien stood behind her, his suit jacket hooked over one shoulder, his eyes boring into hers. He looked tired, his face drawn. But no less heartbreakingly gorgeous.

Her insides performed a slow somersault, then kicked her heart into her throat. She wanted to jump to her feet, rush to him, throw herself into his arms. But she remained seated, frozen, even as her heart soared to giddy heights.

Reaching forward, he removed Xander's phone from her nerveless fingers and tossed it back to him.

A seat miraculously materialised next to her.

He sat. '*Bon soir*, Ana.'

His tone was neutral, his face the impassive mask she'd hoped never to see again. 'H-Hi,' she managed to stutter. 'How was your trip?'

His gaze imprisoned hers. 'Illuminating. And very necessary.'

Charged silence gripped the table. Someone pressed a champagne glass into Bastien's hand. Conversation resumed at a much more frenzied pace than before.

Jumbled thoughts flitted through her head—the uppermost being that Bastien was back. She fidgeted, her heart simultaneously aching and lifting with joy every time she looked at him.

He held up a hand for silence in the room. 'Robin tells me the shoot was a success. I saw the final cut on my way here and I concur. You all deserve praise for a job well done.'

A cheer went up.

'We're going next door to the club. You coming?' Xander asked amid the high-spirited chatter.

'No, we're not,' Bastien answered, his voice low but forceful. 'We're leaving.'

Goodbyes were exchanged. Before Ana could draw breath she was in the back of Bastien's limo, speeding away from the hotel. Silence throbbed for several minutes as the car took them back to the château.

'Any reason you didn't want to go to the club?' she asked, to fill the silence.

His jaw clenched for an infinitesimal moment before he released a breath. 'I don't want to go another day without things being settled between us. But we can go if you really want to?'

Deep apprehension filled her heart. 'Um. No, thanks.'

He merely nodded and returned his gaze to the window. Another five minutes passed. Ana clamped her hands in her lap, hoping to stop their shaking. Her inner quaking she could do nothing about.

'Bastien…' she started, not knowing what to say but knowing she had to say something.

He shook his head. 'Not here. We'll talk when we get home.'

Home.

Ana was sure he hadn't realised his slip, but the Château D'Or *had* become home to her—in a frighteningly short space of time. It was where she'd discovered love and passion. The place where she'd experienced Bastien's kindness and generosity. It was also the place where, given the chance, she hoped to beg his forgiveness.

The car swung through the wide, imposing gates and she finally recognised the foreboding she'd felt the first time she'd passed through them for what it was. Fate—knowing what was in store for her—had been preparing her for the phenomenon of falling in love. She hoped Fate would be equally kind in granting her a chance to make things right with Bastien.

The car drew to a stop at the foot of the château's steps. Bastien helped her out, then immediately moved away.

'I have a quick phone call to make. I'll come and find you shortly.'

Not what she'd expected, but she could hardly complain. Summoning a smile, she nodded and watched him walk away, the sight of his imposing shoulders, his sleek body, balm to her starving, wounded heart.

She drifted aimlessly from room to room, her mind and her emotions churning. Ending up in the tower room, amidst the last of the filming equipment, Ana cast her mind over that last scene.

After years of living in an emotional vacuum her character had been reunited with her one true love, their commitment cemented by the symbol of love he'd carried with him for years—the priceless diamond.

Dared she tempt the fates and hope that fantasy would become reality? The diamond she could do without. All she wanted was for Bastien to—

'There you are.'

The rumble of his voice stopped her wishful thoughts. He came forward, and her heart clenched tighter at the look on his face.

'I wasn't sure whether you wanted a drink or not.' Bastien held out a glass of wine and watched her walk towards him.

His senses roared to life at the sight of her. The four days he'd been away felt like a lifetime. A lifetime during which the fear that he could lose Ana had been a living thing inside him.

For the first few hours after he'd arrived on his parents' doorstep he'd remained in shocked limbo, reliving the bleak memory of Ana walking away from him over and over. Ironic that the one place he'd striven to stay away from all these years had been the one place where he'd been able to find answers that might help him win back the woman he loved.

'I...I'm glad you're back.'

He focused on her, drank her in, imprinted her on his senses. Tried not to reach for her. 'Are you?' He needed to be sure.

Watching the rough cut of the ad campaign on the plane, especially that final take filmed in this room, had lodged a heavy stone in his gut.

His rational mind knew it was acting. But watching Ana in the arms of another man had been...difficult. Difficult? It had been hell!

It had also brutally brought home to him that everything had changed. He was no longer detached, no longer able to hold his feelings at bay.

Their pasts were inextricably linked. And, as much as he'd fought it before, he wanted their futures to be linked too.

All he knew was that he wanted Ana. No. It was more than that. He yearned for her. Against everything he'd fought against...every precaution he'd taken...he'd fallen under her spell. And he was ready to fight hard and dirty if need be.

'Robin tells me you came up with most of the ideas for the ad campaign. That the slogan—"Diamonds by Heidecker...for the Woman Worth Waiting For"—was your idea. Why didn't you tell me?'

Surprise lit her face, followed by a blush. One shoulder lifted in a shrug. 'Because it wasn't. Not entirely, anyway. I just came up with the idea to make it into a…a meaningful story rather than just another run-of-the-mill depiction of a woman wearing expensive diamonds.'

'"A meaningful story"? You mean a romantic story.'

Her chin tilted. 'What's wrong with that? It works, or you wouldn't have given it your seal of approval.'

'I like the idea. What I don't like is the subterfuge.'

A glimmer of hurt crossed her face. 'There's no subterfuge, Bastien.'

'I didn't see your name anywhere on the script. So someone else is taking the credit for your idea.'

She shrugged. 'It really is no big deal, Bastien.'

He stepped closer, drawn like a moth to a seductive flame. 'It is to me. It should be to you. Fight for what you're owed.'

She licked her lips. 'Why?'

'I don't like the thought of someone taking advantage of you.'

'Are you putting yourself up as my protector?'

'Would that be so bad?' he asked.

Her breath caught. Bastien stared down at her, words crowding his brain. She stared back, her brown eyes deep, probing, breathtaking. Every breath, every nerve, every sinew clamoured for her. He wanted to pull her to him, to feel the soft suppleness of her body against his, to hear her breathe his name.

'Thank you for hiring the lawyer for me.'

'It was nothing less than you deserve. I'll always look out for you.'

Her eyes widened. 'What are you saying, Bastien?'

'Do you know where I've been these past few days?'

She shook her head.

'I went to see my parents,' he said. 'I drove through the night to Gstaad. We had a long talk.'

A wave of pain darted over her face as she gazed up at him.

He forced his free hand into his pocket to stop himself caressing the shadows from her face. Deep inside him something twisted, because he knew her pain was for him.

'How...how did it go?'

Bastien tried to will away the pain of that confrontation, tried not to remember the emotion that had clogged in his chest at his father's remorse—*'My weakness destroyed this family...you practically had to raise yourself...forgive me...'*

'It was difficult. There's been so much blame, so much bitterness. I knew it wouldn't be easy, but the time was long overdue to deal with the past. To make things right with my father. To make things right with you.' And with the mother he'd discovered cared deeply for him after all.

Ana thrust her glass on to a nearby surface and came closer, her eyes imploring. 'Bastien, please believe me. I had no idea what sort of pills they were or I'd have never—' Her voice broke.

Unable to stop himself, he reached for her. 'You have to stop blaming yourself, Ana. I don't blame you for that. Neither do my parents. You need to get past that and forgive yourself or we can't move on.'

Tears glistened in her eyes. Her hand fluttered up, almost touched his, but then veered away to rest against her throat. 'Move on? What are you saying?'

'I'm saying the past has overshadowed our lives for long enough. My father has his faults, but he's more than made up for them these last sixteen years. I didn't want to see it because I've been locked away in that cold gazebo all this time. It took your daring me to break me free. As for my mother...' He sighed. 'She knew the pills you gave her weren't headache pills.'

Her eyes widened. 'She knew?'

He gave a grim nod. 'She didn't go to Verbier with the intention of taking her own life. And she called my father within minutes of taking the pills. So there's really nothing to forgive you for. Sometimes in the midst of deep trauma you forget the important things. I forgot that for a long time she shielded me from my father's behaviour. I think that's why it didn't make sense that she would try and take her own life. I lost sight of that, but spending time with her reminded me. I think we've all paid enough, don't you?'

Her nod was shaky. Almost as shaky as he felt, standing there, so close to her, every nerve screeching at him to reach for her.

In the end he decided not to fight it.

'I missed you,' he said simply. 'Did you miss me?'

'I— Yes!'

He gathered her close, kissed her. And everything fell away.

As conversation-stoppers went it was extremely effective. Ana fell into the kiss with the reckless abandon of a skydiver jumping out of a plane.

Except for her there was no parachute. But right at that moment she didn't care. She had Bastien in her arms, his fierce heart beating underneath her fingertips. The fall would come later. Without Bastien's love it would hurt. But for now she would glory in the flight.

By the time he'd carried her from the tower room down the stairs to his suite and kicked the door shut, Ana felt delirious with need. Frantically, she tore at his clothes.

'Patience, *cherie*,' he husked in her ear, before nipping her earlobe.

A deep shudder raked through her. 'I…I can't. I need you,' she gasped.

He stilled her frantic hands, kissing them before bringing them to her sides. 'And you will have me,' he vowed heatedly. 'But first let me undress you.'

His eyes on hers, he released the catch in her belt and dropped it. Then he sank onto his knees. His hands traced her hips, her delicate pelvic bones, squeezed her bottom. Ana moaned, reaching out to steady herself on his broad shoulders as his fingers explored the bare flesh of her thighs. Her whole body hid a morass of sensitive nerve-endings she'd never known existed.

Take the skin above the back of her knees, for instance. Who knew Bastien's hand lingering there could cause her to cry out in pleasure? Or the mid point between her calf and her ankle? He seemed to know her body better than she did.

By the time he eased her feet from her heels she could barely stand. Her dress came off in a rustle of silk. She stood before him in a thong and matching bra.

Eyes the colour of molten steel raked over her. 'I was a fool to say I only wanted one night with you,' he rasped, one hand moving around her to snap the catch of her bra. It tumbled to the ground, unheeded.

'Why?' she croaked.

'Because one night would never be enough, *ma belle* Ana.' He rose and caught her in his arms, locking one hand in her hair to tilt her face to his. 'Never enough.'

He rained kisses all over her face, his mouth almost worshipful. Nonetheless those kisses lit fires wherever they touched, making her senses whirl with desire and, yes, love. What had happened before she'd discovered her feelings had been sex.

This, for her, was making love.

She touched him, revelled in his growl of pleasure when she encountered bare skin. It took a moment for her to realise he was naked; that she was lying on top of him in his bed. The heavy throb of his erection against her belly sent a surge of need through her. She wanted him to fill her body, to fill her heart.

But first she wanted to explore him the way she'd never had the chance to before. Freeing herself from his kiss, Ana kissed along his jaw, nipped the tight flesh. His breath exploded from his lungs, his hands tightening on her back as she kissed her way down his throat, his deep chest. His flat, washboard stomach clenched as her lips and hands worshipped him.

Finally, heart thumping in her throat, Ana felt him against her cheek. She glanced up. Bastien's gaze seared her, an untamed desperation in its depths that caused her blood to surge faster through her veins. Unable to deny herself, she closed her hand over him. His whole body jerked as she stroked him, a deep groan rumbling through his chest and filling the room with arousing sound.

'Ana…' Her name was part plea, part warning.

Daringly, and because she knew the alpha male in Bastien wouldn't let her have this freedom for long, she closed her mouth over him. Ana wasn't sure whether the moan was hers or his. But the feel of him in her mouth, on her tongue, sent her to another level of pleasure so intense she felt her clitoris throb with renewed force.

His gaze broke from hers, his head rearing back as he sucked in a long, harsh breath. Blindly, he reached out and plucked a condom off the bedside table. Strong hands reached for her, pulled her up and flipped her underneath him. His mouth smashed down on hers, tinged with a desperation that bordered on cruel.

He surged inside her with one long stroke, his arm under her hip to hold her still for his complete possession.

Tears gathered behind her closed lids as pleasure rode higher and higher.

When the gathering force of her climax drew closer Ana opened her eyes. Bastien stared down at her, his eyes darker than they'd ever been. Emotion swirled through them, but none she could fathom through the sensational rollercoaster she rode.

It gripped her, surged higher, until Ana knew she couldn't hold back.

'I love you.' She gave up the words that screamed through her soul.

Blank shock covered his face before he closed his eyes and breathed deep. Then, leaning down, he claimed her mouth in another searing kiss, moments before bliss overtook them both. As they slowly returned to reality he gathered her close and breathed strangled, unfathomable words in her ear.

Long after Bastien fell asleep Ana lay awake, desperately trying to stem the fear that she'd just let herself in for a whole load of heartbreak by admitting her feelings.

Deep inside she knew they'd come a long way from sixteen years ago.

What terrified her was that Bastien would never take that last step into love.

CHAPTER THIRTEEN

'BASTIEN, I'M NOT sure what's going on here.'

'What's going on is that I want you. You want me too. Stay with me.'

Ana replayed their simple yet life-changing morning-after conversation as she rose from the bed and walked towards the log fire in the luxurious log cabin Bastien had brought her to in Chamonix.

She had been like a prisoner granted a last-minute stay of execution, and her ecstatic, 'Yes!' had been lost beneath the onslaught of his hungry kisses.

He'd flown them here by helicopter and that 'yes' had echoed throughout the passing days. They spent the mornings skiing and doing her lessons. More than once his patience and gentle attention had brought tears to her eyes. The afternoons, evenings and long nights were spent making love in front of the roaring fire.

A deep blush stung her cheeks as she recalled Bastien asking if she now had a favourite position. She'd felt decidedly wanton as she'd demonstrated which position brought her the most pleasure.

'I can see your blush from here.'

He stood in the bathroom doorway, naked except for the towel he was using on his wet hair.

'It's the fire,' she responded, unable to stop her eyes devouring his perfect male form. He dropped the towel and strode towards her. His teasing grin stopped her heart moments before it began to thunder when he captured her mouth in a slow, devastating kiss.

'Yes, it must be. Because you're all hot and bothered.' His smile deepened.

'I'm not bothered,' she answered feebly as his hands closed over her breasts. His thumbs played over her nipples. Ana swayed towards him, helpless against the drowning rush of love.

But that love was tainted with a niggle of fear that wouldn't go away, a fear that her love would never be fully returned. Sure, he worshipped her body with an intensity that took her breath away, but her confession of love had never been returned. And she'd begun to notice his shuttered expression each time she confessed it.

The need to ask him hovered on her lips as he took her in his arms. Gathering her courage, she leaned back and looked into his eyes.

'Bastien…'

He rested his forehead against hers. 'Unless we want to be trapped here for the next few days we really must leave now.'

Heavy snow had been forecast, and while the thought of being snowed in with Bastien for the foreseeable future held intense appeal, the spectre of her trial loomed.

They hadn't talked about it, but it was there at the back of her mind, growing larger with each passing day.

'Hey, you're biting your lip again. What's wrong?'

'It's nothing.' She tried to step away from him, but he held on to her.

Tender fingers brushed her cheek. 'It's not nothing. Tell me.'

Deciding to shelve the matter troubling her heart for now, in favour of the matter in her mind, she murmured, 'It's the trial. I'm scared.'

He pulled her closer and sealed her lips with a gentle kiss. 'I didn't want to jump the gun until I was absolutely sure, but I heard from my investigators a couple of days ago.'

Alarm spiked through her. 'And?'

'It's not your mother,' he replied.

A burden she hadn't even known she carried was lifted off her shoulders as relief swamped her. The tears that seemed to hover close to the surface of her emotions nowadays prickled her eyes.

'Thank you for telling me.' She gave a small laugh. 'You must think I'm hugely irrational when it comes to Lily. But she's been texting me the last few days.' She'd received many texts from her mother, the last one with a request to see Ana when she returned to London. 'If we can salvage something from our messy relationship...'

'I don't think you're irrational. It's difficult to believe the worst of a parent. And I think we both know what can be salvaged from messy relationships,' he replied.

His voice was solemn, but Ana noticed it contained none of the hard edge of before.

'As for the trial—my investigators will know who the culprit is very shortly. Don't worry about it. Whatever happens I'll protect you, Ana. I promise you.'

Her heart lurched at his words. She paused, then decided to come clean. 'I'm not dead certain, but I think it's Simone.'

His mouth compressed and his arms tightened around her. 'So do I. My people are tracking some video camera footage. We'll have an answer soon. I'm sorry.'

She'd refused to accept that Simone would stoop to such levels, but when she let herself really think about it something about her roommate's perpetual giddy state rang false.

She nodded, her heart sick with sadness. 'I need to go back to London.'

'We'll go together.'

Joy flared inside her, but she was too afraid to give it full flight. Despite the certainty that they'd put the past behind them, that all the old wounds had been cauterised, Ana couldn't get past the feeling that Bastien might never love her as she loved him. She'd still take being with him over losing him completely, but she needed some head space to get her heart to accept it.

'I can do this on my own. You don't have to come with me.'

He trailed a hand down her cheek, then winked at her. 'Did you forget that where you go, I go? After all, I still have to ensure you don't abscond the minute my back is turned.'

She quirked a brow and attempted a smile despite the lingering ache in her heart. 'You left me for almost a week and I was there when you got back.'

He sobered. '*Oui*, you were. And I can't express how much that meant to me.'

She rose on tiptoe, helplessly pressing her lips against his.

With a groan he deepened the kiss, momentarily silencing her doubts.

Bastien's feeling were deep enough...

When he lifted his head, glanced at the clock and imperiously announced that they had some time after all, she let herself melt into him.

'Wake up, *cherie*, we're here,' a deep voice murmured in her ear.

Ana prised herself away from where she'd fallen asleep on Bastien's shoulder on the way from the airport.

She straightened and glanced out of her window at a grey and gloomy London. After surrendering her heart to the Château D'Or, the two-bedroom maisonette she shared with Simone in South London looked dismal and almost alien. It would never be home to her again.

The driver pulled up on the kerb. Bastien started to open the door. She stayed him with a hand on his arm.

'Do you mind if I do this on my own?'

His eyes held an admiration she allowed herself to bask in for a moment.

'*Bien*. I'll go and make myself useful in the office for a while. Call me when you're done.'

She nodded. 'I may be a while. Lily's coming over in an hour, then I need to pack warmer clothes.'

He smiled and reached out to caress her nape. 'Keep those risqué jeans, *cherie*. I've grown quite fond of them.'

She laughed. 'I'll consider it,' she replied, then leaned in to him for a deep kiss.

That niggling voice rose again, cautioning her against falling harder without hope of having her feelings returned. Feebly, she pushed it away.

When he pulled back his eyes were dark and his expression intense. 'You have three hours, then I'm coming for you.' He thrust the door open and helped her out.

Stepping into the frigid air, she pulled her coat around her and held her smile till Bastien's limo was out of view. Dragging her suitcase behind her, she unlocked the front door, dread eating away at her stomach as she entered the flat.

Simone sat cross-legged on the sofa, with Ana's laptop—which she'd bought solely for working on her lessons—balanced on her legs. She was so engrossed in whatever she was doing that it took her a moment to notice Ana in the doorway.

Shock rounded her eyes. 'Ana—I had no idea you were coming back today!'

Ana propped her case by the door and dropped her handbag on the coffee table in the small living room. 'How do you know the password to my laptop?' she asked, her throat drying. The combination was the date she'd met Bastien, known only to her.

Simone shrugged. 'You must have told me when I borrowed it before.'

Heart hammering, she stepped closer and noticed Simone's overbright eyes and agitated breathing. 'No, I didn't. I'm sure of it.'

Her roommate laughed but the sound was skewed. 'What are you saying? That I'm a liar?'

Ana clenched her fists and breathed deep. 'I know, Simone.'

Simone's eyes narrowed. 'Know what?' she demanded, shoving the laptop aside to stand up.

'The drugs. I know it was you.'

Several expressions chased over Simone's face before it settled into pure malice. 'You can't prove it.'

Ana sighed. 'Yes, I can. You made sure you were out of sight of the nightclub's cameras when you put the drugs in my bag but you forgot that it was your birthday—everyone wanted a picture of you, whether you were aware of it or not.'

A flash of fear widened the other woman's eyes but the malice remained. 'You're lying! I was careful...'

'Not careful enough. What I want to know is why?'

Simone rolled her eyes. 'Oh, get off your high horse! Everyone does drugs—but you're too good for the rest of us. You won't even take painkillers when you have a headache. Truthfully, I didn't want to do it. Top-class drugs like that are expensive. But I was warned there might be a raid and—' She froze. 'Are you recording this?'

'Excuse me?'

Simone bared her teeth and snapped her fingers. 'Oh, yes—you wouldn't know how, would you? Because you can't *read*.'

Ice dredged Ana's insides and her gaze went to the laptop. Sure enough, the file holding her lessons was open, along with the phonetic program that went with it.

Anger overcoming the icy dread, she rushed to the sofa and snatched up the laptop. 'How dare you—?'

'Don't bother denying it, Ana.'

Ana stared at her. 'Were you going to let me go to jail for something *you* did?'

Simone shrugged. 'Why not? Everything comes so easy to you—the contracts, the private jets, the billionaire boyfriend. Does he know, by the way?'

That disturbing thread of doubt reared its head again. 'Yes, he knows. He's okay with it.'

Surprise mingled with fear on Simone's face but she quickly regrouped. 'Yeah, keep telling yourself that. I'm not owning up to the drugs thing. I'll tell everyone you were in on it. It'll be your word against mine. You think his company will survive another scandal? Especially if you remain his girlfriend?'

'Forget it, Simone. I'm not going to jail for you,' Ana said, despite her heart thundering with a different kind of fear as Simone backed towards the door.

Her roommate ran out of the room. A few minutes later Ana heard the front door slam. She wasn't worried about Simone getting away. Bastien had told her that the police had been alerted and his own investigators were tracking her.

Bastien…

The knock on the door made her jump.

Her stomach twisted at the thought that it might be Bastien even as her heart thrilled at seeing him again. Swallowing, she opened the door.

Her mother was dressed from top to toe in white vintage Chanel, her face perfectly made-up and her hair twisted in an impeccable bun.

Mingled desolation and pain scythed through Ana. Stepping forward, she let her mother in. 'Hello, Lily.'

Everything she'd thought she'd heard in her mother's voice recently was reflected in Lily's face, albeit warily.

'You look distressed. What's wrong? Is it…? Do you want me to leave?'

Ana shook her head. 'No, it's not you. I've just found out who planted the drugs.' She quickly summarised her conversation with Simone, then glanced at her mother as she accepted her halting commiserations. 'What's going on, Lily? You seem… different.'

Her mother's laugh was strained as she followed Ana into the living room. 'You mean less of the nightmare you grew up with?'

Ana shrugged. 'Your words, not mine.'

For the first time in her life Lily seemed nervous. 'I…I started a drug rehabilitation programme last month. One of the steps in the programme is making amends. I wish I could say that I didn't need a bullet point on a piece of paper to make me realise I've been the worst mother in the world to you. I just… Once I started down that destructive path I didn't know how to make things right.' She stopped and firmed her trembling mouth.

Ana closed her own gaping mouth and stared at her mother, hope spreading its wings again. 'I…I don't know what to say.'

'Please say you'll give me a chance? That you won't write me off completely?'

Ana's heart squeezed and she blinked back tears. 'I won't write you off.'

Her mother's sigh of relief was audible. 'I don't deserve it, but thank you.' She fidgeted, glanced around, then eyed the suitcase by the door. 'Are you going away again?'

'Yes, Bastien will be here in an hour. What?' Her insides jerked at the wary flicker in Lily's eyes.

'I spoke to Philippe two days ago.'

'Bastien's father?'

Lily nodded, her blue eyes darkening with pain. 'Part of the making amends process… Couldn't be avoided. Ana, he told me about Bastien's visit.'

'Yes, Bastien went to see them. I think we're all ready to put the past behind us—' She stopped when her mother shook her head.

'I really hope for all our sakes that's true, but Philippe is worried about Bastien. He thinks he's carrying a lot of hurt from sixteen years ago. I'm sorry, I know you have feelings for him, but I want you to be careful.'

Don't confuse love with sex or duty…

The voice was a loud clamour in her head and in her heart. And, try as she might, Ana couldn't stem the growing fear that she was indeed jumping without a parachute.

'I really hope you find joy and happiness where I sowed only pain, and I don't want to see you hurt.'

Lily's eyes bored into hers with a look Ana had thought she'd never see from her mother.

Affection.

Her throat clogged and she stood. 'Don't worry about me. I'll be fine.'

Her mother rose too. 'That was the other thing I came to tell you. I've re-signed with Lauren. Apparently there's still hope for modelling work for women of a certain age. If you need me to stay on as your manager…'

Ana shook her head. 'No, I'm giving up modelling. I'm hoping to work with Papá for a while.'

Lily's eyes clouded over with tears. 'Your father is next on my list.'

Ana stepped forward and grabbed her mother's hand, swallowing a sob when hers was caught in a tight hold. 'I'm proud of you…Mother.'

Lily hugged her tight, then moved back. 'Call me…when you get to wherever you're going.'

The moment her mother left Ana sagged numbly onto the sofa, her gaze frozen in the middle distance.

Her mother had inadvertently confirmed her worst fears—that she was looking for love where none existed. Bastien had shown her gentleness and consideration. He'd made love to her as if she was the most precious thing in his life. But the fear that he'd never take the next step and love her was one she could no longer deny.

Her phone buzzed. Willing her heavy limbs to move, she fetched it from her bag.

It's B. R u OK?

Tears filled her eyes. She was willing to bet Bastien had never sent an abbreviated text in his life. That he was bending to accommodate her touched her heart even as it cracked painfully.

Wiping her tears with the back of her hand, she activated her keypad and carefully typed in: Yes. C u in 1 hr

Fingers shaking, she closed the application and turned off her phone. Pain twisted like potent poison inside her. Giving in to the raw anguish, she burst into tears, her soul ripping into a million little pieces.

She wasn't sure how long she stayed on the sofa. It might have been close to an hour but it felt like an eternity. When she had no more tears left she slowly rose, grabbed her suitcase, went into her room and upended the contents onto her bed. On automatic, she refilled it with sensible, everyday clothes. The rest of her things she'd arrange to be packed and put into storage when she could think straight.

She blanked her mind to the fact that she would never see Bastien again, never feel the intensity of his lovemaking or feel the gentleness afterwards when he cradled her in his arms.

The pain of their violent separation would come later...when she was miles away.

But she'd come too far, been through too much, to settle for a life without love. They'd bared so much to each other in the past few days. Surely if Bastien loved her he'd have told her by now? Recalling his silence when she'd confessed her love, she bit back a dry sob and heaved her case off the bed. She retrieved her bag and laptop from the living room, breathing a sigh of relief that she still had her passport.

Taking one last look at the flat, she headed for the door.

The travel agents were a few minutes' walk away. Ana entered the building and came out fifteen minutes later, clutching a plane ticket.

CHAPTER FOURTEEN

BASTIEN'S TEETH GRITTED together as he fought to remain calm—fought against the primal urge to roar against the pain that ripped through him every time he thought of Ana.

He felt weak, debilitated, as if struck down by some alien disease. Even his heart wasn't sure whether to beat fast or slow, so it alternated between the two, constantly robbing him of breath. He thought of what he'd do when he found her. First he'd kiss her, and then he'd shake her until he got an answer. Then kiss her again—

He heard laughter as he approached the dusty, dilapidated trailer in the middle of the Colombian jungle. Familiar female laughter. His heart thundered and the surge of joy through his veins was so thrilling, the knowledge that he'd found her at last so heady, he smiled before he could stop himself.

Mon Dieu…three long weeks he'd searched for her.

The deep male voice that joined in the laughter stopped Bastien dead in his tracks. There was a man in there…with Ana. *His* Ana.

He wrenched at the door before his thoughts coalesced. It refused to budge. He smashed his fist against the frame.

The laughter ceased.

'Open this door, Ana. *Now!*'

Footsteps drew closer. Before the latch had turned fully he wrenched it open.

She was dressed. That was the first thing Bastien made sure

of the moment he saw her. She was dressed—albeit in the tiniest pair of shorts known to man and a halter-necked top so thread-bare it was almost see-through.

'Bastien! What are you doing here?'

Her slack-jawed astonishment drew his gaze to her mouth—a mouth he hadn't tasted for what seemed like a lifetime. Hunger pounded through him, its fierce bite instant and relentless.

He ignored it, his gaze moving to the man who rose from the chair near the window. A tall, lanky man with long brown hair dressed in a distinctly hippy-type outfit.

'Who the hell are *you*?'

His snarl made the other man's eyes widen. Bastien's satisfaction wasn't great, but it was welcome nonetheless. Ana's horrified gasp barely registered because he was busy devising ways to break the other man's limbs.

'Bastien, you have no right to speak to my guest like that.'

He extended a hand. 'Bastien Heidecker. Apologies for my rudeness. And you are…?'

Before the other man could answer Ana stepped up beside him. 'Adam is my tutor.'

'Tutor?' Belatedly Bastien saw the books spread over a small table by the window.

'We were just discussing the Tudors and Henry VIII's fond-ness for excess,' Adam offered.

Any emerging regret for his rudeness towards Adam immediately evaporated when Bastien saw the way he smiled at Ana. Every muscle in his body tightened at the adoration in the man's eyes.

He bared his teeth. 'If I'm not mistaken, Henry also had an extreme fondness for beheading.'

Taut silence settled in the trailer. Adam cleared his throat. 'I'll…er…leave you two alone.'

The door had barely shut before he reached for her. 'Are you sleeping with him?'

The need to know burned a wide and jagged path through

him, although at the back of his mind he asked himself how he'd handle it if she said yes.

'What? Are you serious—?'

He plunged his mouth down on hers, firstly to shut her up, but mostly because his need had become so gut-wrenching he couldn't think straight.

Her mouth opened up beneath his. His senses sang as he renewed his acquaintance with the potency of her kiss. He folded her into his arms, his hands rediscovering the exquisite curves he'd dreamed about day and night for endless weeks. Her soft breasts pressed into his chest, their heavy weight and hardened peaks a reminder of all he'd desperately missed.

He'd barely scratched the surface of his hunger before she pushed him away.

'You didn't answer me. What are you doing here?'

He stepped back and raked a hand through his hair. 'What the hell do you think? You left me without an explanation after you texted that you'd see me in an hour. *An hour*, Ana. It's been three weeks!'

'I know how long it's been,' she muttered.

'Tell me why? What did I do?'

Ana stared at him, standing so tall, proud and heartbreakingly gorgeous. Weeks of restless nights when her dreams had been so vivid that on waking to find she'd only been dreaming she'd burst into tears more than once didn't do justice to the reality of him. And, even though his face lacked some of the vitality she loved, he was still the most magnificent man in the world.

A magnificent man who would never return her love.

She turned away.

'You didn't do anything, Bastien. It was me.'

Bastien stopped himself from reaching for her again, compelling her to look at him. 'Whatever it is, tell me. I can take it.' A blatant lie. He wouldn't be able to take it if she rejected him.

A delicate frown creased her forehead. He wanted to smooth it away, to touch her once more. Her skin had darkened in the Colombian sun, making her more alluring if that was possible.

Her beauty enthralled him, made him want to kneel at her feet in worship. But he needed to keep his wits about him. Needed to stay sane. Because he was fighting for his life. Fighting for the woman he loved above anything else in his life.

Her tongue snuck out to wet her lips. 'What we had was great but it wasn't enough. I'm sorry.'

His vision frayed and he gripped the back of the chair. 'What are you talking about?'

Her finger traced a delicate path on the rickety table. 'I want more.'

'I will give you more. Just tell me how.'

She stared at him for a few heartbeats, then her lids descended, her lush lashes shielding her eyes from him. Unable to stand not touching her, Bastien moved and tucked her hair behind one ear. Her breath caught.

'Bastien, I can't tell you how to *feel*. If you don't already feel it…you're better off without me—'

'No, I'm *nothing* without you! What we had… Ana, it was the closest thing to heaven that I've ever known.' Her eyes widened. Bastien fell deeper, even as his desperation grew. 'I don't know why you left but you told me you loved me once. I hope that one day you'll love me again—the way I love you.'

Ana's heart stopped, somersaulted, and then banged with crazy abandon against her chest. She told herself it was the heat in the cabin that made her light-headed, but hope told her it was something else.

'You love me?'

Bastien nodded. '*Oui*. I'll do whatever it takes to make you love me again—'

'I never stopped.'

'You never—'

'No, and *you* never told me how you felt.'

He grimaced. 'I did. You're the love of my life, Ana, *amour de mon coeur*.' He repeated the words he'd first said three weeks ago.

Her eyes widened as recognition dawned.

'I felt safer saying it in French because I was a fool and thought that way I wasn't risking everything.' He gathered her closer. 'But I aim to say it in every language there is—starting with English. I love you, *ma belle* Ana.'

Her heart soared. When he gathered her close she didn't resist. His kiss was hungry, demanding, possessive. And she loved it. He backed her onto the tiny cot she slept on and came down over her.

'Here?'

'Have mercy on a poor man, Ana. I've been without you for three long weeks. I can't take another single moment without you.'

Her sigh of pleasure was all the answer he needed to continue.

Later, in the equally tiny shower cubicle, he pulled her wet hair to one side and washed her back. Although there was more kissing than washing. Not that Ana was complaining.

'Marry me,' he muttered against her shoulder.

Ana froze. 'No. You *can't* want to marry me.'

His head snapped up, his eyes narrowing. 'Credit me with knowing my own mind, *mon coeur*. I love you. I wish to spend the rest of my life with you. Marriage is the next natural step. Ana, I would be proud to have you by my side every day for the rest of my life. You've forged your way successfully through life and I'm proud of everything you've achieved. I would be even prouder to call you my wife.' A touch of vulnerable pain clouded his eyes. 'Why did you leave me, Ana?'

'I thought you didn't love me. After everything we'd been through, I thought if you loved me you'd have told me. When you didn't...'

His eyes turned smoky. 'I will tell you every day how much I adore you. And if that doesn't work I have a few aces up my sleeve.'

'Oh, really?' Her smile felt as if it would split her face as she moved into his arms.

'Really.' He grinned, then sobered. 'I met your father an

hour ago. He grilled me thoroughly before he showed me where your trailer was. I think I passed his potential son-in-law test. But if that doesn't work… Remember the tower room the night I got back?'

Intrigued, she nodded. 'One of the crew members had left a camera on. It recorded our conversation, but more importantly it recorded you melting into my arms, kissing me like I owned your soul.'

'You do. But blackmail, Bastien? Seriously?'

He grinned. 'Not as powerful as a sex tape, but I'll use whatever ammunition I have so you'll never leave me again.' He sobered. 'You've believed in yourself, thrived despite all the setbacks you've received. Take this last step, *mon amour*. Marry me.'

'I can't. Not yet. I've signed up with my father's programme. I need to stay in Colombia for two years.'

He merely shrugged. 'Then I'll stay with you. I can work from anywhere in the world.'

'But—'

'Marry me,' he repeated, his purposeful tone making her heart soar. 'Let me stay here with you. You can teach me Spanish as we pick through the bones and I'll teach you whatever you need to learn. Of course that means *I* will resume tutoring you. Adam will have to go.'

Tears filled her eyes. 'I love you, *mi corazón*. Of course I'll be your wife.'

His kiss was long and deep. When he lifted his head the emotion in his eyes moved her soul. 'I don't deserve you, Ana.'

'But you've got me all the same. You're mine and I'm yours. *Siempre*.'

'For ever.'

* * * * *

JBS_2014